BEAR'S STRENGTH
Guardians of the Fae Realms: Book 3
JL Madore

Copyright © 2020

**JL Madore**

Cover Design: Gombar Cover Designs

Note: The moral right of the author has been asserted.

This is a work of fiction. Names, characters, places and incidents either are the product of the author's imagination or are used fictitiously, and any resemblance to actual persons, living or dead, business establishments, events, or locales is entirely coincidental.

**Bear's Strength: Guardians of the Fae Realms**

**JL Madore** -- 1st ed.

ISBN: 978-1-989187-47-0

# CHAPTER ONE

Brant

*I*t's four o'clock in the afternoon when we step off Hawk's sleek Gulfstream G650ER jet, at a private airport outside of Portland. Hawk's pilot taxied us right inside the hangar, so despite it pissing down rain, we're free to stretch our legs while the airport Welcome Wagon does their thing.

Hawk takes Kotah, his younger sister, Keyla, and Doc over to meet a few of his hand-picked security staff waiting by the office door, and Calli, Jaxx, and I wander.

"Hey, Lukas," I say, nodding to the military-fit, right-hand mage of our avian mate. The guy has proven solid from the get-go and after he saved our asses with his magic dome of impenetrability during the missile attempt on our lives, I've learned to respect him as part of the team. "Hawk said the warehouse in Eugene was a bust. Did you find anything we can use? Anything that leads us to where those teens are being hidden away?"

Lukas meets my knuckles for a bump and tilts his head from side to side. "Nothing inside, but a local investigations officer skimmed the garbage bags from the closest dumpster and found a couple of shipping orders made out to the FCO. She's tracking the manifest info and accounts now. Maybe we'll get lucky and they'll lead us to something we can use."

"Cool. Where can I find her?"

Lukas points to the second of three, black SUV trucks parked outside the open doors of the hangar. "She's working off her laptop and phone."

I take that as my cue and head out.

*Damn.* It's really coming down. I duck my head, scoot into the deluge, and dive into the back seat as quickly as I can manage. The door slams behind me and I'm still brushing my hands down the slick layer of water on my arms when her scent hits.

*Shit on a stick.* "Hey, Hannah," I say, offering her what I hope is an easy, charming smile. "So, you're the local IO Lukas mentioned, huh? When did you switch to investigations?"

Hannah Gantley, a redhead witch with fairy blood from the Seattle office, twists around in the shotgun seat and smiles. "If you'd called like you said you would, you'd know the answer to that, B."

*Okaaaay.* So, I may have found too much enjoyment in Hawk's two past-lover fiascos with Calli. It seems the universe has a sense of humor and is goosing me in the ass.

"A lot has happened in my life too, beautiful. Did you hear about the rise of the phoenix? I'm one of her guardian mates. I'm the chosen ursine."

Hannah draws a deep breath and shakes her head. "You don't carry the scent of a mated male. You sure you want to stick with that story?"

My bear growls loud and long. *No.* My scent isn't merged as a claimed mate. Jaxx, Kotah, and even fucking Hawk have mated Calli over the past week and a half, but here I am, the charmer, stalled in my tracks and on the outside looking in. "There's nothing wrong with wanting to take things slow."

Hannah snorts. "You taking it slow? You *do* remember our first sextacular meeting, right?"

"Of course, I do." I had her long legs wrapped around my hips twenty-five minutes after we locked eyes across the dancefloor. "That was different. That was a bar crawl hookup. No strings. No complications."

She tilts her head toward the hangar. "So, your mate-in-waiting is strings and complications?"

"No!"

"That's what you said."

"That is not at *all* what I said," I say, my bear growling at the offense of even implying I would say such a thing. "*Shit*, forget it. I came to find out about the leads from the warehouse but it was obviously a mistake."

I reach for the door handle and Hannah reaches back and grabs my shirt. "Relax, Bear. I'm fucking with you. Tall, dark, and military over there told us almost nothing about why we're here but your place as one of the chosen guardians is hardly a secret. Call me childish but twisting the screws to you took the edge off you dumping me."

I shake my head. "Hannah... I never dumped you. I'm sorry. I didn't realize you thought we were anything more than a good time when I was in town."

She stares at me for a moment longer and bursts out laughing. "Okay, still fucking with you."

I flop back against the leather seats and curse. "Can we please fast-forward past the fucking with me part and focus on what you found at the warehouse? My bear's not in full control right now and you're testing my focus."

Hannah sobers and shrugs. "Sure. Right after you tell me what's really going on with the warehouse and why it's so hush-hush."

"If it ends the torment, done deal. Last fall, I took down three different kids with off-the-charts, unique fae affinities. When I followed up on them a month or so ago, I found that they'd been erased off the face of the earth. It's a thorough wipe. Their parents know nothing about any of them, my files were altered to omit mention of them, and according to the records in the Fae Palace, they never existed."

"Their existence is completely erased?"

"Yeah. It was made to look like Hawk Barron is behind it, but that's not the case."

"How can you be sure—"

"Because he's another of our mates." I wave off her skepticism, surprised how sure I am now of his innocence. "Trust me, I explored that avenue and it's a dead end. As our bonds grow, so too does our sense of each other. Hawk's a hard-ass but he's also a patriot to all things fae."

"So, three kids are missing, and you thought they might be in that warehouse?"

"No. Fourteen kids are missing, and we don't know where the hell they are. Every time we dig deeper, we find that it's worse than initially suspected. That's why we have to move on this... and why we have to keep it quiet. Fourteen kids are depending on us and the enemy is our own people."

Hannah purses her lips and frowns. "Okay, so here's what I've found."

～

*Calli*

My phone vibrates in my pocket and I check the text from Brant. Text? Where'd he go? I look around the shiny white hangar and don't see him. Alright, so I open the text.

*Full-disclosure moment, beautiful. You asked for a heads-up if you meet a female from past indiscretions. I can't remember what we agreed on. Hannah. FCO co-worker. Nothing important. Don't fireball me.*

I show Jaxx the screen of my phone.

My jaguar arches a golden brow. "Yeah, I'm not sure where we landed on that minefield either. I say good on him for being proactive and to err on the side of not getting his balls sautéed."

I chuckle. "You make me sound like a jealous maniac."

"Says the female who threw fireballs at Hawk's head and almost burned down the Fae Palace."

"Hey, both the Council Minister and that ebony-haired bitch taunted me. I understand as well as the next girl that you four are gorgeous and virile and that three of you have past relationships. I simply don't take being ambushed well."

Jaxx still doesn't look happy about my request for full disclosure. I originally thought his discomfort stemmed from him wanting to save his own ass, but then I clue in. Jaxx isn't like that. My Texas cowboy is a southern boy, born and raised. "It offends your moral code of discretion to tell me, doesn't it?"

He shrugs. "Yeah, more than a little."

After Hawk exposed my damaged past to them, it was Jaxx who offered a clean slate option. A roadside rebirth. We agreed to start over from the moment I resurrected from human roadkill to a wildling phoenix destined to unite two realms. If I ever learn how to transform into my phoenix form.

Big if on that one.

"Hey, kitten," Jaxx says, pulling me against his chest. He chucks my chin and I gaze up into his stunning turquoise eyes. "Don't be sad. No one in my past can touch what you mean to me. If you need every detail to feel secure in us, I'll tell you. I just won't like it."

*Huh?* "Oh, no. My mind wandered. I was thinking about not being able to shift and letting down both worlds."

The tension in his body eases and he envelops me in his hold. "It's only been two weeks. The rest of us took a decade or more before we could call our animals with any accuracy. Stop being so hard on yourself."

He presses a chaste kiss on my lips and the growing tension inside me eases off… a little.

Jaxx's skin glows with a beautiful golden tan, and he smells like fresh air and spruce trees. When he's this close, it doesn't matter that we played in the shower this morning after a wild and wonderful twofer in our bed.

He's mine and I hunger for him—insatiably.

His eyes grow hooded as he breathes deep, and a sexy purr rumbles up his chest. The deep-throated timbre vibrates within my cells and a glorious pang of desire hits. My nipples peak as a rush of wet heat dampens my panties.

"You know better than to purr for me in public, puss."

Jaxx bites his lip and his gaze searches the space. "You speak as if it's voluntary. When my mate is HAF, I have no control."

"HAF?"

"Horny as fuck. And the scent of it makes me crazy."

*Horny as fuck?* And here I thought I was playing it cool.

I giggle as he grabs me by the wrist and pulls me down a side hallway and into a small lounge. It's got a love seat, a glass side table with a stack of magazines, and most importantly a lock on the door. He leaves the overhead fluorescents off, locks the door, and seizes me into his arms.

With Jaxx, everything happens in a blur of sexy. Cool air hits my thighs as my pants are shucked down my legs. I manage to get my shoe off and one foot pulled from my pant leg while he undoes his jeans.

That's all the time I get.

He grips the fleshy rounds of my ass, and then I'm off the floor and my shoulders bump the back of the door. I'm pinned against his hips, my core open, and my ankles wrapped around his thighs.

"Yesss," he growls as his erection slides deep. "Damn, I love that you're always wet and ready for me to glide home."

To accentuate his point, he pulls out to his swollen tip and then slides home once, twice, and by the third time, I bite my lip to keep from gasping. This isn't our bedroom, or somewhere we can settle in. As soon as Hawk finishes with airport security and getting Keyla sorted, we'll be on the move.

"Be quick," I gasp, gripping his broad shoulders as I bump and bounce behind the weight of his thrusts.

"You first," he growls, pulling me off the door to walk us over to the courtesy loveseat. He sets me on my feet, pulls out, spins me to face the wall, and gives me a shove to bend me over the arm of the sofa.

"Bossy, boy." I laugh. He spreads my stance with a toe on the inside of my ankles and impales me in a solid thrust from behind. I collapse forward and gasp into the cushion.

"You don't seem to mind my alpha comin' out." Jaxx laughs and builds his penetrations to a pounding rhythm. Bent with my bare ass in the air for a quicky in an airport lounge would've been uncomfortably risqué before my transition.

Now, the animal inside me craves these wild moments.

"Best view *evah*," he says, his voice as deep as his cock inside me. I hear the wet pop of his thumb being pulled from his mouth and my core weeps. "You said to be quick, right?"

The pressure of his thumb playing at the rim of my ass sends off an electrical pulse in my cells. He's playing but my orgasm builds wildly in anticipation. From behind, I feel every inch of him inside me so much more keenly.

The head of his cock hits something delicious deep in me and, with the added succulence of his thumb pressing against the tightly closed flesh of my bottom, I shudder. "Gawd, yes."

More of the rough fucking. My body rocks with every slam of his hips. I press my hands into the plush fabric of the sofa, being careful not to let my fire escape and burn the couch. That would be awkward.

My release builds hard and fast. My intimate folds stretched wide. My inner muscles grip and grab at the ridges of his slick cock. A sharp keening heats my core and I fan the flame, coaxing it to grow, to take me, to ignite like wildfire.

His breath is catching behind me and I love that he's exerting himself. If I can be a workout for these guys, strip me down and sign me up. I push back against the force of his thrusts, my palms spreading on the seat, my resistance making his hips slam harder. Deeper.

His thumb circles. He's done playing now. He forces his digit past my resistance, and I buckle onto my elbows.

The nerve endings he strokes send a shot of fiery pleasure straight to fuel the wildfire. "Oh, gawd, Jaxx... so good."

I'm lost. I press my face forward and cry out, my pleasure caught in the cushions. His thumb slides and strokes while his breathing tightens behind me.

I know what's coming next and my orgasm builds and starts to pulse, waiting... wanting...

The purr that rattles from his chest isn't the playful one he makes in public. This purr is his jaguar about to pounce. It's the end of his resistance. His release about to let loose.

The primal rumble ignites my release. I'm surrounded by the smell of our juices, the sinful pleasure of his thumb probing and playing, the slap of flesh on flesh mixing with his cat's claim of ownership. My jaguar is alpha and possessive.

And by him... I love being possessed.

My body shatters. I come hard, panting into the couch as his breath hitches behind me and his hips slam home and stay thrust tight against me. With a bruising grip on my hips, he grunts and growls, pressing deep into my pulsing womb.

*Yessss.* It's a wildling thing, something about mating heat, but one of my favorite parts of sex with these guys is feeling the heat of every spurt and spray of cum inside me.

My mate is marking what's his.

It's magical and feeds my phoenix with strength and an unshakable sense of belonging. The guys get off on it too.

It also alters my scent so there's no doubt to any other wildling, or fae with a sense of smell strong enough to detect it, that I'm taken. That I am theirs.

The soft knock on the door has us both straightening. "It's only me," Kotah says from the other side of the door. "Hawk is finishing up. We're ready to go."

"Thanks, sweetie," I say, sagging. I wish we had ten more minutes so we could enjoy the afterglow, but we don't. I grab my pants pooled around one ankle and hustle toward the adjoining powder room. "Give us two minutes."

# CHAPTER TWO

Jaxx

*J*escort Calli back into the open hangar and we merge with the stream of bodies heading to the trucks. With my hand on the small of her back and my mark fresh on her skin, all is right in my world. I'm so freaking in love with her it's ridiculous. Every time I'm inside her, I'm humbled. Her wildling side grows stronger and more confident by the day. Her phoenix is close to emerging—and she's going to be spectacular.

She is already spectacular—she just doesn't realize it yet.

Kotah returns from the farthest SUV and meets us the threshold of the open hangar door, umbrella in his hand. The rain has eased to a misty drizzle, the sun pushing at the seams of the silver sky to make an appearance.

He kisses Calli's cheek and flashes me a sexy-as-fuck smile. "Apologies. I didn't mean to rush you."

I smile and shake off the apology. "Nah, we're good."

"You're incorrigible," Hawk says, rolling his eyes.

Calli lets off a burst of laughter and accepts Kotah's hand. The two of them climb into their seats and settle in.

I turn to Hawk, who seems more than a little put out and close the truck door for a private word. "Seriously? You're pissed we stepped away for fifteen minutes?"

"I'm pissed that we're in a crisis, speaking with business professionals, and my mates are acting like horny teenagers when we're all adults."

I throw him a cocky smile. "No. You're an alpha who doesn't like to share—especially with another alpha. What's the harm here, Hawk? We got bored. We took a moment. I bet you no one else even noticed we disappeared."

"Six hours after you two went at it at Northwood Hall. Try a little restraint, Jaguar."

I turn my back to the truck and lower my voice. "This mating is bound to be different for each of the five of us. You can choose to address our mate alignment by making travel arrangements and enjoying a palm-warming stroke and choke alone at night. That's not me. I choose to lavish her with the love and acceptance she never got and build her confidence. If you spent more time inside her, you'd realize how much the connection coaxes out her wildling side."

His square jaw flexes as he grits his teeth. "That's all well and good, but does it have to be every five minutes?'

"She had the urge and I had the time."

"And isn't it nice for you that you don't have any other demands on your time?"

I see it then, what comes off as territorial jealousy is rooted in fear. Hawk had sex with Calli once to mate her, but he has no faith in the mating. I'm spending my time showing Calli what we can be, and he doesn't see it.

He sees himself getting left behind.

"Hawk, this isn't a case of may the best man win. We all win here. It's Musketeer time. All for one and one for all. Aligning as mates isn't us with her. It's all five of us."

He stiffens and my cat growls long and low.

"Dammit, avian. We won't mount you the moment you let your

guard down. You're not open to male-male with us. You've made that clear. Despite what you think, you're not all that. We can resist you."

Hawk's attention flickers to the SUV pulling away and snaps back into CEO mode. "Now's not the time."

He steps off, but I match his move and grab his wrist. "I'm just sayin', let us become what we're meant to be as mates. Friends. Partners. Maybe lovers in the sense that we all focus on Calli. Just don't isolate yourself."

He glares at my grip on his wrist and I release him. I get that he's only a team player if he's the captain and the coach, but that won't work here. There are two alphas in this mating, and we need to work that dominance shit out.

"You don't know me or what motivates me."

I nod. "Agreed. And if you keep up your bullshit, we never will."

∼

*Hawk*

When the reinforced titanium gate hums shut behind the truck's bumper, the one in front of us releases and begins a slow swing to allow our entry. The Portland compound I rented for our stay boasted state-of-the-art security features, a seven-bedroom main house, a four-car garage with three-bedroom loft above, and a nine-acre treed lot trimmed with hotwire and alarms.

"Wow." Calli's eyes pop wide as we drive up the winding lane. "Look at this place."

Brant snorts in the shotgun seat beside me. "Bribing our female won't win you any congeniality awards. avian."

I shoot him a sideways glare. "And if the decision was left to you, where would you house the phoenix savior of the Fae Realm, the Prime in Waiting, and the Prime Princess? A Super 8? How about a Day's Inn? I hear they've got a complimentary continental breakfast bar."

"Har-har," Brant says, making a face. "This is ursine territory. My point is that I can get us housing anywhere along the Pacific coastline without drawing attention."

"I didn't draw any attention. I simply rented a house. In my circles, there is nothing odd or out of the ordinary for a wealthy male and his entourage to move into a compound while they're in town. Trust me, Bear. I've built my empire in information security. I know how to do discrete."

We round the last bend of the drive and face the glass and stone house head-on. It's a stunning monument to organic architecture with fluid lines and natural materials. It's large enough for our group, private, and secure.

"This will do nicely."

Brant busts out laughing. "Yes. It's very discrete."

I shift the truck into park, shut off the engine, and bail out. It's close to dusk and the gas lamps lining the walkways have lit. Pressing the fob on the keychain, I pop the back hatch and meet everyone at the back tailgate to grab our bags.

Jaxx grabs his and Calli's duffels and they head across the paved courtyard toward the house. Brant is still grumbling as he pulls his bag from the back and lumbers off. Kotah slings his bag over his shoulder and presses a hand to my arm.

The kid's smile tightens when he registers my reaction and I curse inwardly. It's a reflex I need to work on. "Thank you for taking such good care of our group, Hawk." A rush of calm and warmth tingles into my system from his touch. "For the house, the security arrangements for my sister, and the lengths you go to for our well-being... all of it."

"You're welcome."

Despite what Jaxx said, I'm not isolating or being an ass. I'm doing my part in this mating like him. I'm just not doing it with my dick.

Kotah's smile widens and I have an idea of what's coming. The guy keeps hugging me, even after I told him to stop. I think I manage to bury my instinct to back away... it doesn't matter. Right when I think he's going to move in and get personal, he pulls back and pats my arm. "We're lucky to have you. Thanks for all you do."

Kotah peels off, leaving me anxious and feeling weird. Am I off-kilter because I thought he would hug me or because he didn't? Fuck me. This mating shit is confusing.

I shut the truck hatch and curse myself.

I thought accepting the mating with Calli would set my head on straight and I could put this chaos behind me. It helped with the insanity of a throbbing perma-erection, but that's it.

*Dammiiiit.*

I swing my duffle higher onto my shoulder and follow the others. Lukas is smoking with his team beside the garage and I lift my chin in greeting. "Give me five minutes inside and then we'll see where we are."

"Take your time," Lukas says. "We're waiting on intel. Likely closer to fifteen before I have answers."

I nod and head inside.

The side entrance opens into a breezeway mudroom and I sit on the wooden bench to unlace my boots. Once inside, I take my bag up to the second floor to see where everyone is staking their claims.

"We're in here," Calli says, gesturing for me to join her in one of the secondary bedrooms.

I follow her inside and frown at her bag on the queen-sized sleigh-bed. "This isn't the master. The master has a king. Why wouldn't you guys pick the biggest room?"

"Oh, they did. When I said we're in here I meant *we*, us, you, and me." She rushes forward as I step back. "Don't bother arguing. Jaxx and I make and take time whenever passion strikes. Kotah and I will be here getting him sorted on his Prime duties while you and the FCO gang are out on missions. Brant wants to wait and romance me without a crowd. That leaves you and I setting aside time."

I'm about to drop my bag on the bed but remember how she snatched it up and held me for ransom during another bedroom argument much like this one. "We can't sleep together, Calli. The last time we did, you woke up choking and fighting for your life."

"No, that was the *first* time we did. The last time, you took one of your pills and nothing happened. I got to snuggle into you for the night. Then, in the morning, you got up, kissed me goodbye, and went to work."

"You make it sound so domestic."

"Other than there being five of us in this marriage, us being fae wildlings, and one of us being the next king of the realm, we're totally run of the mill."

I laugh. "You should set yourself up with Jaxx and Kotah. They'll be better company."

She shakes her head and the light catches the growing copper streaks in her golden hair. "I need this, Hawk, and I think you do too. I need to feel like we're growing closer together not further apart."

"What about Brant? You haven't even mated him. Save the seduction speech and shift your focus. There are enough bedrooms in this place to woo him and make it official."

Closing the distance between us, she takes my bag and tosses it on the floor. Then, she pushes me back to sit on the bed. I expect her to climb into my lap but instead, she straddles my thighs and rests her arms over my shoulders.

The warmth of her body melts the coldness inside me like it always does. She wriggles closer and we're pressed together from our groins to our chests to our lips. She bites my bottom lip and it's unapologetically rough.

When she releases the tender flesh, she brushes the sting with her kiss. "This is our room—yours and mine. You get to be the boss out in the field. I get to be the boss of whose bed I'm in. I'm not a prize or a treasure to be bartered. I'm a person and I have my own ideas about who I want to sleep with and why. Got it?"

My cock pinches in the confines of my pants and I groan. Desire has a way of convincing even the most dominant male to submit. I'm so close to buckling and letting her control me it's astonishing. I can't. It's not safe for her or me. Still, I'm not going to win by turning her down either.

"If I agree, will you let me go?"

"For now, yes."

"Okay, yes. Though, I think the danger to you is—"

My argument is blocked by her tongue in my mouth. I've never been a fan of bottoming, but it's different with Calli. Jaxx is right about one thing. She's finding herself, exploring her strengths and her wants. For some reason I can't explain, she wants me... even knowing who and what I can be.

Her passion is a heady thing.

She's solid and warm and unapologetically aggressive.

And then, she's gone. I blink up and see her rolling to her feet and putting distance between herself and the edge of the bed. As she backs away, her bosom rises and falls in a breathless attempt at control. I'm glad I'm not the only one who gets carried away.

I swallow. "Abandoning ship?"

She chuckles. "Keeping my word. I said I'd let you go, so consider this me setting the stage for later. Be safe out there, broody. And while you're searching for missing kids and mired in lies and hostility, know I'm waiting for you to come home to me."

I rise from the mattress, my biological hunger for my wildling mate unsated and noticeable against the front of my pants. I think about Jaxx's comment about her needing to feel our acceptance to grow into a fully transitioning phoenix and give the jaguar credit.

He's more than a pretty face.

Stepping up to her, I clasp her hand and press it firmly against the bulge behind my fly. Leaning close, I brush her cheek with mine and whisper against her neck. "You up for a little sexplay, Spitfire?"

She grinds the heel of her palm against my cock and suddenly, my life outside this room seems far less important. "Anything you've got in mind."

Fuck she's trusting. "While I'm gone, work on your hand-to-hand and shifting with Kotah—no sex. Then take a nap. When you wake up, text me and I'll give you further instructions."

"Will they be sexy Dom instructions?"

"They will. Now, workout, nap, and then text. Show me how obedient you can be if you try."

"Will you punish me if I'm bad?"

I arch a brow. "No. I'll rescind the offer if you're bad. You *want* me to punish you. I will only reward you if you do as I ask."

Her smile is nothing I deserve. "Sir, yes, sir."

Fuck me. I'm in serious trouble with her.

*Brant*

The delivery label Hannah found in the dumpster led us back to a home-builder bulk store. The run of the mill purchases didn't get us anywhere and neither did the FCO corporate card because it expensed everything in Hawk's name. Where we did luck out was that the purchaser of the lumber, drywall, wire, and light fixtures used the same corporate card for all his local purchases.

While Hannah tracks the number down looking for our bad guy's identity, delivery addresses, etc. Jaxx puts his hacking skills to good use and tracks the locations of all the purchases in the area so we can get an idea of their home base.

"Got it." Doc comes into the office unfolding the corrugated flaps of a map. My closest friend from my sleuth, the ex-military medic turned bodyguard has been my rock through this mating chaos. He knows me and isn't afraid to step in and voice his concerns if he thinks I'm losing focus.

I need that sometimes.

I point to the empty meeting table and we set ourselves up. This mansion has a fully equipped office and despite me talking smack to Hawk about showing off and over-doing it, his foresight always seems to come in handy.

"How stupid can this guy be?" Jaxx asks.

I scan the monitor screen over Jaxx's shoulder and smile wide. "Honestly, I won't complain. The Black Knight might be strong and mysterious, but his minions' overconfidence works in our favor. Doc, grab some colored pens, and Jaxx, print that off for me. Let's get an idea where this guy is."

The laserjet hums to life and I snag the sheet of paper as it spits out. "All righty, now we're cooking with gas. First point, Starbucks 122nd Avenue where it meets Airport way."

Doc traces a finger over the map and makes a green dot.

"Next one, Costco. 4849 NE 138th Avenue."

It goes like that until we exhaust the list and are looking at a cluster of dots along the Columbia River along the 205 heading toward Washington State.

*Ding.*

"Hello, there," Jaxx says, hustling back to the desk. "Okay, I put a flag on the card. It just got used at a public storage on 136th."

"Good enough," I say, grabbing my flack vest from over the back of the chair and slinging it on. "Forward the directions to me—"

"Screw that," Jaxx says straightening from the desk. "I've transferred it to my phone. Let's go."

I'm about to argue when Hawk joins us. "Go where?"

Jaxx and I rush past him and head toward the breezeway to grab our shoes. "That credit card just pinged. It's not far and I'm going. You might need EMS for those teens."

Hawk grabs his boots and gets with the program. "You can go if you stay in the truck until the scene is cleared."

"Fine. As long as I go."

Boots on, Jaxx tucks his soul crystal into his shirt and gives Calli a quick kiss. "Love you, kitten. See you soon. If we're not back, wish Kotah luck with his call to the Palace."

Hawk finishes with his laces and squeezes her hand. "Remember what I said, Spitfire. Workout, nap, text, reward."

Calli bites her lip and nods. "Yes, sir."

*Okay, ew.* I have no idea what that's about but am so focused on rescuing those kids I don't care. As I pass her, it hits me. The other mates are working to advance their relationships while I'm holding out for the perfect moment and looking in the opposite direction.

I bend down to brush her lips with mine. "I'm sorry I'm so preoccupied, beautiful. I'll do better, I promise."

Calli cups my jaw and then runs her fingers into the wavy lengths of my hair. "You're doing fine. Be safe, Bear. The lives of strangers aren't worth yours. Not to me, anyway."

# CHAPTER THREE

Kotah

"First round we'll do shirts against skins," I say, returning to the grassy lawn at the back of the mansion. Straight from the kitchen, I hold up our weapons. Doc and I are the attacking force while Calli and Keyla are the defenders in training. "Each of us will fight until a mortal wound is struck."

I offer them four rubber-ended baking spatulas in different colors. "Choose your weapon wisely my friends for they are the only thing between you and your enemy. We'll consider the handles neutral but the ends both cut and burn. A straight stab to a vital organ is a kill."

Keyla arches a brow and chooses first. "Red, the color of spilled blood."

"Well, then." Doc snorts and reaches forward. "Black, the color of death."

Calli is next. "Orange, the color of raging fire."

I look at the one in my hand. "That leaves me with green the color of… frogs. Don't ask me how that's an advantage. I can't think of a good one and frogs are cool. Fun fact. They can jump over twenty times their body length. That's like a human jumping more than ninety-eight feet."

"Okay, that is impressive." Calli laughs, pointing her orange spatula at me. "You're going down frogman and as for death," she shifts to Doc, "I'm a freaking phoenix. Death doesn't scare me. I will rise again."

Doc laughs and we all face off and drop into first positions... "Ready... Go!"

Over the past weeks, one of my truest joys has been to work with Calli each day and witness her skills develop. She's gone from a reactive scrapper to a strategic sparring partner.

She's not ready to take on a gang of hostile drow on her own yet but she could hold them off longer now than she did that first day we met her.

The four of us parry and swipe and jostle for supremacy, settling into a rhythm. This is fun. More fun than I've had in a lifetime of people either judging me or pandering to me.

A red spatula slices through the air by my ear and I duck and shift my footing to keep both Calli and Keyla in view. My sister is classically trained as I am, but, "Palace life has made you soft and slow, little sister."

Keyla laughs catching my arm with the tip of her red rubber. "Sizzle sizzle, brother. That's going to leave a scar."

"Doc, where's my backup?"

"Flaming stab wound to the base of my spine," Doc shouts from where he's lying on the grass. "Death is paralyzed until the next round."

The girls are closing in, so I dive roll into an open spot and regroup.

"Fancy frog moves won't save you, my love."

I catch Calli mid-air as she dives full-bodied at me. Cushioning her descent, I roll, absorb the hit of our bodies colliding with the ground, and lay her gently on the grass. The spatula to the spine seals my end. "Who's soft now, big brother. We knew you'd fall for the heroic save routine."

I laugh, pressing Calli into the grass to claim a kiss before rolling to my feet and pulling her up. "But you sacrificed one of your own."

Calli giggles. "Shirts still won. Go, girls."

Doc joins us looking abashed. "Yep. Chivalry did me in too. Wolf. We obviously need to suppress our more gallant instincts when sparring with these two."

I wink at my mate. "Not possible. Now, should we mix up the teams or rematch."

Doc laughs at that. "Rematch! One hundy percent."

*Brant*

Despite me being the driving force behind tracking our lead and finding the only connection we have with the Black Knight, Hawk all but benches me. When we arrive at the storage units, he orders everyone to park behind the building across the road instead of moving in. It's bullshit and it makes my bear insane to take orders from him.

"We need to scoop this guy up," I say.

Standing in a huddle outside our truck, Hawk responds to something he hears on his comm system and looks to the gathered officers. "Two of you to the office for unit verification and intel. Lukas, you're on the target. I want him tagged. Two more on the roof for observation. I want these fuckers, boys and girls—all of them. Don't tip our hand."

Lukas, Hannah, and their crew disperse to carry out the orders from on high.

"And what?" I say, annoyed to be sidelined. "We're going to sit in the truck with our thumbs up our asses?"

Hawk folds his arms and leans against the driver's side door. "If that's what does it for you, go ahead, otherwise, be patient."

"You're going to lose him. How many operations have you actually been on? You're a corporate suit. Leave this to the people trained in the field."

Hawk scowls. "Well, I'm glad to see you're not letting your prejudice get in the way of your ignorance, Bear."

"Fuck you."

Hawk opens the truck door, leans across the seat and hits the release for the glovebox. When it opens, he pulls out a spare comm set and tosses it at me. "I get that you're pissed, but I'm far more experienced at this than you. There's a seventy-four percent higher chance of learning what we're dealing if we choose surveillance over interrogation."

"That's lame. I know how to get answers from people."

"Some people, I'm sure. And if it comes down to intimidation and brutality, your muscles and growl will be put to good use. Until then, watch and learn."

"There are innocent lives on the line."

"All the more reason to temper strategy with expedience. We'll get to the source as soon as possible. We'll learn more from this guy if his guard isn't up. Be patient."

Patience is not my strongest virtue, especially when Hawk's the one leading the band. Still, I can be a team player. I guess he and I resolving differences here is good practice for the whole mating thing too.

"Trust me," Hawk says, forcing a smile. "You'll get your chance. We'll stick with Lukas for the tail and you can stay in the thick of things. For now, it's brain instead of brawn."

"And what if whoever is in that storage unit makes us and gives us the slip. Then we have nothing."

"Not going to happen," Lukas says, returning from his deployment. He rounds the corner with a weapon that looks like a paintball gun mated with an assault rifle. "I tagged his pant leg and his car. Even if he makes the tail and leaves us in his dust—which he won't—he'll show up on our scope."

"Unless he strips down and streaks through the streets in his gitch," Jaxx offers.

Lukas concedes that possibility. "But even then, he won't be able to blend. Streakers generally gain notice." He turns the screen of the mobile tracking unit and points. "We're up and rolling, folks."

"Is he blue or red?"

Lukas makes some fine-tuning adjustments and then shows me again. "He's the blue dot. I'm red. This handheld unit is synced up with me."

"Man," Jaxx says. "Investigations officers get all the best toys. I've been bitching to my team leader for months to get better storage straps for the oxygen tanks in my rig. I'm fighting for nylon straps and they get state-of-the-art James Bond gadgets?"

That's actually true. The spy gadgets and cool guns are one of the reasons I wanted to transfer from being a field enforcer to investigations. The only drawback is that IOs don't get to bust heads nearly as often as enforcers.

Hawk frowns at Jaxx's rant. "Well, now you know someone a little higher than management. Write me a report on what's working in the field and what's not. I give each department a ridiculous budget to ensure FCO teams have every tool they need available to them. There is no reason why you couldn't have had new safety straps."

Jaxx smiles. "Yeehaw, it pays to sleep with the boss."

Hawk rolls his eyes. "We ain't sleeping together, feline."

"Okay," Lukas says, pointing to the screen. "We're on the move."

Hawk opens the front door of the truck and jumps into the driver's seat. As the engine rumbles to life, he touches the earpiece of his comm and it lets off a soft *beep*. "Team two, once our target is clear from the site, I want that unit swept from top to bottom. Do the fine-toothed comb routine and find us something we can use."

*Calli*

I wake, curled around the thick silver and chocolate coat of my wolf, my arm hooked under his front leg and tucked under his neck. My wolf gets the grand prize for cuddling. He's like a living body pillow. It's decadent. Pressing my face against his neck, I breathe in the forest scent his coat always carries and his omega magic feeds my soul.

How did I ever survive without Kotah in my life?

"I love you, sweet prince."

He shifts back to the man I adore and gathers me against his chest. The magic of his shift tingles across my skin. I don't know if I'll ever get used to the magnificence of it. The whole shifting thing still blows my mind.

"I love you, too, *Chigua*."

I smile at his endearment and rub my hand over his navy polo shirt. *Chigua*... he's called me that since the beginning. In his family tongue, it means greatly beloved war woman. It is a title of honor for women who exhibit true heroism on the battlefield. I love that he thinks of me that way. It makes me want to live up to his image of me.

"Did you have a good rest?"

I prop up on my elbow and sit my chin in the palm of my hand. He brushes my hair back from my face and the touch of those two fingers against my cheek is so tender my heart melts. "I didn't realize I was tired, but yeah, I slept."

"Your body is undergoing massive changes and with all the training, traveling, and sex, Hawk was right to insist you take a nap. We don't want you depleted."

"I'd never be too tired for you, Wolf."

He chuckles and kisses my cheek. "I meant you need to be rested if danger comes knocking."

"Oh, well, yeah. Knowing us, it won't be long until the sky is falling once again."

Kotah's gaze is a warm caress as he studies my face.

"What is it, sweetie?"

He shrugs. "It's silly."

Okay, now I'm really curious. I snuggle back down and rest my cheek on his shoulder, curling my arm over his chest. "Tell me. Silly or not, I want to hear it."

He presses his lips to the top of my head and breathes me in. Jaxx does that too. It's a wildling mate thing and it seems to offer them comfort. "When I was a boy, there were a few moments when my family wasn't cold and dysfunctional."

"I'm glad to hear it."

"They were rare, granted, but in those brief moments, I used to memorize exactly how I felt so I could draw on it later when things went back to being strained."

"And that's what you were doing? Memorizing me?"

He lifts my arm to his face and runs his nose against my forearm. It tickles as he draws my scent into his lungs and presses his lips to the inside of my elbow. "Yes."

"What does that look like to you. What's important?"

"Mmm… the weight of you, here, laying in my arms. How our scents merge. How the light picks up the highlights your phoenix is adding to your hair. How strong my wolf feels next to you—both lethal and loving."

"That's nice."

"It is."

"I want to feel like that too. Part of the reason I'm training so hard to shift is so I can feel like I'm strong for you too. I hate that my vulnerability puts any of you in danger. I want our quint to be five strong warriors fighting side by side, not four strong warriors protecting their mate."

"Don't worry. Every day your phoenix grows stronger and more skilled—she's magnificent. When she's ready to show her full, fiery self, you'll be the one protecting us."

"You say the sweetest things." I lift my head to kiss his jaw. "You are my foundation in all this, Kotah. The subtle strength that gives me faith in everything we're building."

I mean for my praise to make him happy. The sadness in his gaze breaks my heart. As the omega, he's the one who eases us. I have to remember to take better care of him because he won't do it for himself.

"What's wrong?"

"With the Prime appointment looming, I'm afraid I'll lose my place with all of you. I don't want to fail any of you. I don't want to be separated from you."

"You won't," I say, sliding my arm back to hold the soul shard that came to him in the Northwood grotto. "You are our spirit, remember. Our very essence. You are the breath we breathe, the subtle breeze to cool off hot tempers, the gale-force strength when trouble arises."

"And what happens when my duties as Prime take me to the Palace? Who am I then?"

"You're still you." I kiss the shard and set it on his chest. "Whether we're in Oregon or North Dakota or Lebanon, Kansas, we'll be right there with you. If you think being called to the castle will sever what we're building, you haven't been paying attention. Besides, it's not only me who's laid a claim. I've seen some hot and heavy longing between you and Jaxx."

Kotah's chest jiggles beneath me as he chuckles. "I am enjoying exploring that mating bond. Jaxx is…"

As he trails off to think, I supply a few of my own observations. "Sexy and wild and possessive."

"Yes."

"A great kisser and a powerhouse fucker."

The growl that rumbles beneath my ear is sexy as hell. "He's a very addictive lover."

"Preach."

He goes back to running his lips up the inside of my forearm. "Does it bother you, at all?"

"What? You and Jaxx?"

His chin brushes the side of my head as he nods.

"If I remember correctly when I asked that exact question of you at the Bastion, you said, 'Calli, we are to be a mated quint. You stand here smiling, relaxed, and sated. How can that be a bad thing?'"

He chuckles. "And your response was, 'Well, it's not for *me*, but I want to make sure there's no tension and that no one feels left out.'"

Man, he slays me. "I don't feel left out. I get how addictive Jaxx is and think it's awesome that our mating claim is taking hold on different channels."

He exhales a deep breath and I realize he was genuinely concerned about upsetting me. Silly wolf. "Speaking of the different channels of our bond, how goes your quest to break through Hawk's barriers?"

The mischievous sparkle in his deep, chestnut eyes sparks my curiosity. "What? Are you holding out on me?"

Kotah eases out from under me and sits up. "I used one of Mama's suggestions today. You know how I'm trying to strike a familiarity of touching him, even in the most platonic ways?"

I sit up and cross my legs, nodding. "Yeah, and you're washing him with ease to soothe his annoyance."

He nods. "Well earlier, I did the same thing but retreated without hugging him. I played hard to get."

"And?"

His triumphant smile is far too delicious. "I felt his confusion as I backed away. Part of him was disappointed. He objects to the contact but not entirely."

"Operation Mating Quint is taking hold." I hold up my palm and we high-five. "Time to text our broody bird."

I reach over to the bedside table to grab my phone and Kotah places a hand over mine to pause me. "Maybe you should have some privacy? From what you said, Hawk has something intimate to share with you."

I bite my lip. "Good point. *I* have no problem sharing everything with you, but he might consider it a breach of trust. I have to protect what little ground I've gained with him."

"Agreed. I'll go find my sister. We are supposed to video chat with Raven about palace duties in half an hour. You can give me the broad strokes later and let me know how things go." Kotah leans in and kisses me before rolling off the bed. "Good luck."

# CHAPTER FOUR

Brant

"Well, I guess crime does pay," I say as Lukas and I push through the heavy shrub and peer over the stone wall that secures the private estate our bad guy led us to. "This place is even more discrete than the place we're in."

Lukas pops a brow. "You consider our mass tribute to steel and glass discrete?"

I chuckle. "No, but your boss does. Long story. So, are we going in, or what?"

Lukas looks up to the dark, dusky sky. "We'll have the full cover of darkness in ten minutes. I'll find our entry point and wait. You go back to the truck and get night vision goggles for me and an infiltration kit."

I have no idea what's in an infiltration kit, but why bring that up. I'll figure it out. "Right. Back in a flash."

As it turns out, a flash is six minutes and I find Lukas perched in the crux of a massive old tree twenty feet from the stone wall.

"You want me up there?"

He shakes his head and steps out into empty air. The magic surge to control his descent makes the hair on my arms stand on end. The guy has juice. I wish I knew how much and where it comes from. Trusting someone in the field demands a level of confidence you don't achieve by holding your cards close to the vest.

I doubt Hawk and I will ever get there.

"Earth to ursine. You with me bear?"

I blink and shake the cobwebs loose. "Yeah, sorry. I'm good. Here. Is this what you wanted?"

Lukas takes the backpack from me and takes a quick boo inside. "Yep. All good." He pulls out the set of goggles I tucked in there and secures them on his forehead. "There's a magical field blanketing the first twenty feet inside the entire compound. The top of the wall is fully amped to blow the top of our heads off. And inside that, the security team has cloaking and are invisible."

"Holy fuck," I say, my mouth hanging open. "So, what's our plan?"

Lukas breaks into a wide smile. "That depends on how adventurous you are and if you're up for a running leap of faith. Oh… and how far you think you can throw me."

*Hawk*

I'm scrolling through the email report of what team two learned at the storage depot when my notification tone for Calli *pings*. We haven't texted much since the days and nights I was separated from them while running the Monster Rights Conference last week. What I intended to be a way to keep tabs on what was happening at the palace in my absence became a fun distraction. Bantering with Calli, I found myself enjoying her spark.

In-person, she often infuriates me.

Remote conversations, though, I found… easier.

Close to her, my hunger and dominance weigh in and I lose track of what I want to say and why. Teasing texts and sexting give me the distance I need to stay in control.

"What's that smile?" Jaxx says from the passenger's seat beside me. "Did we get a lead?

"What? Oh, no. Calli's texting me."

Jaxx nods. "Ah... good. I'm glad she puts a smile on your face. Listen. I'm gonna stretch my legs and grab some fresh air. Take your time."

The jaguar bails out of the truck and steps onto the grassy shoulder of the road. It's almost full dark. Lukas and Brant will soon be able to move in. I take the moment of inactivity and give Calli's message my full attention.

*Workout complete. No sex. Nap over. Well-rested. What now, Sir Barron?*

So eager. For a female who fights me at every turn, she's certainly agreeable when it comes to wanting me to be her Dom in the bedroom. I have a feeling it might be the only place in our mating life where she surrenders herself to my wishes. With her, I'll take what I can get.

*Open my duffle. There's something in there for you.*

*A present?*

*Something like that.* I wait while she goes to grab it. Glancing into my mirrors, I check that all is quiet and I'm not going to be killed while distracted.

*Okay, got the box. Am I opening it?*

I chuckle. I pictured her yanking it open on sight. Points to her for playing the submissive game better than I expected.

*Yes. Open it.*

*A kink kit... lol. Just what I wanted.*

*Some things you'll recognize, others might be new. I purchased each with you in mind. It's a beginner kit, so there shouldn't be anything there you find too objectionable. Use Incognito and research the ones that intrigue you. Eliminate the ones that don't.*

*Homework?*

*I expect a full report outlining your thoughts and curiosities tonight when we turn in... if you're game.*

*Duh... I'm so game. I'm wet just thinking about it.*

I shift in my seat and check my surroundings. Night is overtaking the gray of dusk. I can't sext right now despite my cock throbbing behind my fly. *It's delayed gratification for both of us, Spitfire. Don't satisfy your need. Let it build. In fact... do you see the black toy that looks a little like a snowman with a silver bottom?*

*Yes.*

*Insert it as instructed, turn on the vibration to its lowest setting. I'll take it from there. Give Kotah the remote and tell him I'll text him instructions.*

*Kotah? Don't you trust me?*

*To not seduce him and let the pressure off? No.* I laugh to myself, picturing her scowl. *Consider it a team project. I'll tend to you as soon as I can get back. Later, mate.*

*Later, Sir Barron.*

I call up Kotah's number and quickly explain. *I'll control it remotely. She can't take it out and she can't orgasm. Watch her. She's tricky. I hate to cock-block you, Wolf, but don't satisfy her no matter how horny she gets.*

*Lol. You can count on me. Looking forward to this.*

I clear my screen and grab the door handle to get out and join Jaxx. My phone pings with another text from Calli.

*Slid in like a warm, wet dream. Hurry home, broody. Your mate needs you to fuck her.*

I read it twice and groan.

Before claiming her in the shower, I didn't grasp the carnal pleasure possible with a mating bond. Letting off inside her... feeling my cock squeezed by her pussy while I marked her inside and out... fuck, it was transcendent.

I now understand how she went from being skeptical and scared to grasping the reins of that bond within the span of a week. I could spend months inside her, marking her and making her cream in every position imaginable and still never sate my desire.

I reread the text. *Your mate needs you to fuck her.*

Yeah. I need that too.

The night air feels good on my heated flesh and I tip my face up to the cloud-shrouded moon. Rounding the front of the truck, I pull out my cigarette case, light one of my hand-rolled sticks of delight, and join Jaxx in the shadows.

"I see your call went well," the jaguar says, gesturing to the front of my pants.

I'm about to toss out a snipe when I catch myself. Instead, I shift my footing and adjust my cock. A long pull on my smoke helps gear down my sex drive and my annoyance at having another alpha male comment on it.

I turn my head away from him and exhale the exotic succulence. "I suck at small-talk, Jaguar. I survive on two modes of communication, dominant or hostile. I'm working on it but we're not there yet."

"I feel you. It's a lot. I get that."

*Hmph.* "Doesn't seem to slow you down any."

Jaxx shrugs and points to my cigarette. "Can I bum one?"

I get him set up and slide the silver case back into my pocket. "I didn't know you smoke."

"There's a lot we don't know about each other." He stares out at the darkness and the heater flares as he takes a pull. "Dayum, avian. This is nice. What's in it?"

"It's my own blend of Turkish and Orient tobaccos laced with a hint of CBD to take the edge off."

We stand together, smoking, and I feel like I should say something. Jaxx always seems to know what to say to put people at ease. That's not one of my gifts. "I wish I was better at this, Jaxx. I excel at a great many things but not... this."

His head cants as he searches my expression. I don't know what he thinks he sees, but his smile makes me squirrely. "And what is 'this' to you, Hawk?"

I wish I knew. "I pride myself in anticipating what's coming at me next. This mating blindsided me. I don't know how to plug into what we're supposed to be building."

"The big question is do you want to?"

I chuff. Two weeks ago, the answer would've been a vehement 'fuck no'. Last week it would have been 'it won't work'. Since bonding with Calli... I'm struggling to figure out how to make it work.

"So, you want it to work?"

"I do."

"We have to mean more to you than the celebrity of bein' chosen for the quint and the political gain of bein' mated to the next Fae Prime. The five of us need to align as one. Your claim on Calli is a start, but for this to work, you have to want the rest of us in your life too—however that works for you."

I exhale heavily. "I'm a loner and an aggressive, driven alpha. Having other males around me as equals isn't something I'm prepared for."

"If that's all it is, relax. It'll come. Just don't freeze us out in the meantime."

He makes it sound so easy. "I'm not sure if you noticed but my closest friend is my security officer and my last girlfriend was my personal assistant. I only know how to be a boss, Jaxx. Friend and mate are alien concepts."

He exhales a sweet-smelling cloud of blue-gray smoke and I smile. It never fails to ease my roughest edges. "The first step is learning to be at ease with us. Us here, chatting and having a smoke like this… this is good stuff, Hawk."

I search his expression to gauge if he's fucking with me.

Nope. He seems sincere.

"We can hang out for drinks, talk about mate troubles, even meet chest to chest for a hug if the moment warrants it. It won't mean anything more than that. Kotah, Brant, and I are clear on where the line is drawn in your sand. It'll be a lot easier for you to be yourself around us once you trust us to respect your boundaries. You get to do you, Hawk. It's cool. We're cool."

Fuck, in the light of the moon, the turquoise of his eyes practically sucks me in. I don't know why it affects me. I don't do guys. Never have. Never wanted to.

I pull my gaze free. Trust in the boundaries, eh? Isn't that what I've asked of every female I've played with? Kink and BDSM is all about mutual respect and trusting that your partner will uphold your limits.

I never thought about it like that, but *that* scenario, I understand. "I appreciate that, Jaxx."

My comm activates in my ear and I quiet to hear the update from Lukas and Brant. "We're going in."

~

*Calli*

With the vibrating snowman tucked inside me, I leave our bedroom to find Kotah. At first, I take the stairs slowly, but then realize, my little guy is secure enough that I don't have to worry. And he's a fun little guy... sending little horny zings to all my girlie parts.

Kotah meets me at the bottom of the stairs. His Cheshire grin tells me that Hawk has already imparted his instructions. He holds out his palm and I hand him the controller. "On low. Good girl. How does it feel?"

I close my eyes and focus. "I knew I liked vibrators before but this is different. He wriggles a little, rubbing my insides in a sexy way."

Kotah draws a deep breath and his wolf growls. "I love the scent of your arousal. It's pure octane in my veins."

My nipples are peaked, and I bring his hand up to cup my breast. He tests the point with his thumb against the cotton of my shirt and I shudder. "Holding back until Hawk gets home is going to be torture. Between the anticipation, the toy, and the mating heat, I'm raring to go."

Kotah backs me up one step and takes advantage of the height difference to lean straight forward and trap my nipple between his teeth.

"Oh, yep, that's going to get me into trouble."

My wolf chuckles and blows a hot breath through the fabric before straightening. "Then we better stop. This is Hawk's first step in engaging you as a lover. We must not disappoint him, or as you said, we'll lose ground."

I laugh and poke my nipple back down. There are other people in the house. I can't walk around nipple-tipped. "We mated, so it's not exactly his first step. He did claim me in the shower."

Kotah gives me an indulgent smile and shakes his head. "You seduced him when he was naked and vulnerable. He succumbed to your advance and his overwhelming need. This little game of his is him including us in his world and his plans. His trust will be hard to win. We must prove to him we can follow his instructions no matter what."

"Agreed." I prop my arms on his shoulders and link my fingers behind his head to play with his braid. I press my lips to his as a quick offering of solidarity. "Now, tell me. Is everything ready for your call with Raven? Does Keyla have her questions ready?"

"Yes. And Raven is wonderful. She'll know what we need to know to satisfy my palace duties."

I touch the soul shard where it hangs against the hollow of his throat below his royal tattoo banding. "Well, whatever it takes, we'll make it work. Whether we're on the road, at the palace, or at Northwood, this quint stands with you. No mate gets left behind."

He lifts his chin and straightens. There are moments when he looks every bit the part of his royal appointment. "Come. Let's get this over with. I'd much rather focus on Hawk's games than my father's."

He takes my hand and tugs me off the steps, his words playing in my mind. "Do you think your parents will keep playing political games with you? You accepted your appointment and have committed to your duties. What more could they want?"

Kotah chuckles. "How little you understand the self-importance of my soul-sucking parents. There is no end to what they want. Ever. Nothing I ever give will be enough."

A buzzer rings and the two of us follow the sound into the office. Doc is already there, his attention focused on the monitor that shows the security cameras of the front gate.

"We've got visitors."

"Who," I ask, rounding the desk to get a better view. "Seriously? Cut the fucking cord, lady."

The window of the back seat is down and Kotah frowns at his mother's haughty glance at the camera. "See what I mean?" he says, letting off a heavy sigh. "Never enough."

Doc looks at Kotah and shrugs. "Your call, Wolf. We don't have to let them in."

Kotah chuckles. "Unfortunately, Mother isn't one to give up. If she has something to say, there will be no peace until she says it. Release the gate."

# CHAPTER FIVE

Brant

*W*hen we're sure the cover of darkness is on our side, Lukas opens the comm link and tells Hawk, "We're going in." Then, he tests the strength of the branch we're perched on and gives me the green light.

I've thrown a lot of males in my life but usually, that was in the heat of some kind of fight or rescue. I've never shotput a mage for the sake of distance. "You sure about this?"

Lukas dips his chin and grins. "Believe it or not, this isn't the strangest thing I've asked a guy to do on this job."

I decide the fewer details on that the better. "Okeedokee. Are you looking for a lob or a line drive?"

"A lob. Then give me a solid minute and do a flying skydiving leap. Don't worry about the freefall. I'll take care of the rest with magic."

"If you can take care of the rest with magic, why not go with that from the beginning?"

"Because of the magical field. I need to be beyond the twenty-foot perimeter before I call on my powers or we'll trip their security measures. Trust me. I've got this."

I wish I knew what this guy's specialties are, but hey, in for a dime in for a dollar. "Okay, fasten your seatbelt." I grab him by the collar of his flack vest and his belt at the back of his pants. He crosses his arms, grips the shoulder straps of his combat vest, and stiffens.

When I lift him off his feet and assume his weight, the limb we're on lets off a crack.

"That's not comforting at all, is it?" Lukas says. "Okay, we get one shot at stealth and this is it, Bear."

One shot... and my footing is threatening to give way from under my boots. Awesome. Urging my bear to the surface, I take a couple of deep breaths, tighten my grip, twist back... and then uncoil, launching Lukas into the night air.

The next crack of the branch is much more threatening.

I bend my knees, waiting to see if I drop to the ground below. Lukas's trajectory looks promising. Honestly, I'm impressed. He's getting good distance and pierces the air like an arrow shot from a compound bow.

When I lose sight of him, I listen for his landing but get nothing. Well, nothing but the micro-cracking of the branch beneath my boots. "Okay, I'm going," I say, looking down. "Don't get your bark in a bunch. You're giving me a weight complex."

The tree cracks in response and the branch starts to bow.

"Oh shit." I lose track of my count at forty Mississippi but am out of time anyway. As the branch gives me one final fuck you, I take a running leap and dive over the stone fence.

Even with the strength in my legs, my body mass is too dense to get far. Twenty feet is a big ask without firm ground under the soles of my boots. With a snapping twig ejecting me from the tree, it's a no go.

Almost immediately, I sink through the air like a stone.

My arms are still above my head from my jump when something clamps tightly around my wrist. The almost silent whoosh-whoosh of wings has me gaping at the enormous owl carrying me across the compound toward the house. When we reach the main building, the impossibly large bird dips lower and drops me onto a rooftop patio.

I absorb the landing and roll to a crouch, straightening… right next to Lukas. The mage has his hands up and is casting. The energy of his magic tingles like Pop Rocks on my tongue.

I dust off my hands and shake out my hair.

As I watch, the owl shrinks back down to normal size and reclaims his night. "Cool trick," I say, thoroughly impressed. "You must clean up at birthday parties."

Lukas waggles his brow and pulls his night vision goggles into place. I've got north and east. You take south and west. We need a guard count, possible exits from the main house, how many outbuildings, and any idea where they might be keeping the kids if they're here. Meet back here when you're done."

I don't need night vision goggles. Bears see fine in the dark, though I'm still not sure what to think about the security team having the ability to cloak. That sucks.

"Whistle if you need me," I say, turning to go.

Lukas nods. "Same."

*Kotah*

Keyla has enough time to run upstairs and put on a dress before Mother's car stops in front of the four-car garage. She's rushing back down, sweeping her hair up into an elastic as the sound of closing doors echo outside. Calli and I decided not to change and to receive our guests as is. My mother can take us or leave us—preferably the latter.

"Why is she here?" Keyla hisses, straightening her skirt.

"Why does she do anything?" I say, not bothering to hide my annoyance. "To prove to us she can."

Calli curls in at my hip and kisses my cheek. "Could—past tense. You are not her suppressed little boy anymore. You're a man now—*my* man. You're the Prime in Waiting and outrank her. She doesn't get to be queen over you. She holds no power to control you other than what you give her."

I love the confidence in Calli's declaration, no matter how naïve. "Technically, you are correct, though it doesn't work that way. Mother has a knack of ensuring her point of view reigns supreme. She's accustomed to great power. She won't stand to lose that—especially with Keyla and me."

"Tough titty."

Keyla chuckles. "Please use that phrase when the subject comes up. Mother will love it."

Calli sticks her tongue out at my sister and I couldn't be more in love with either of them. Keyla for taking on the role of my shield against the palace politics and Calli for standing as my champion and claiming me—and by extension my sister—as her own.

Doc looks back to ensure we're ready and when we nod, he opens the door and points the way in.

My mother, Raven, and two palace escorts make their way inside. Keyla rushes to take mother's shrug and welcome them. I'm about to step forward when Calli groans and grips my hip tighter.

"Calli? What is it?"

With her face pressed into my shoulder, she licks her lips and clenches her eyes tight. "Oh, gawd. Now is not the time for Hawk to be playing with his app."

I burst out laughing, then cover my mouth and meet my mother's censure. "Nakotah, have you forgotten how to welcome a guest into your home?"

"No, Mother. Once again, you simply caught us by surprise." Biting back my amusement, I sober. "But, since you brought up the topic of social courtesy, you might do us one. Now that I am Prime in Waiting and mated, it's best if you let me know when you intend to stop by. That way, I have a chance to let you know if we are receiving."

Mother looks from me to Calli and back to me. "Receiving? I am your mother. Is this her doing?"

"In the sense that I value my privacy with my mates, yes. Otherwise, no. Since you forced my hand to be sworn in, I now hold a position of elevated status. These drop-in ambushes end now."

I pause and breathe in the glorious scent of my mother's fury and catch the sweet succulence of Calli's arousal blooming. Life is good.

Whether Calli's heat is stirring from me being assertive or Hawk's vibrator massaging her core, I don't care. It's a glorious moment and one I commit to memory.

"If you'll excuse me," Calli says, starting to ease away.

I chuckle and capture her wrist. Hawk trusted me not to let her out of my sight to release. I won't fail in my duties.

"Not so fast, my love. Stay with us so you can ask your questions while we have our meeting. There will be tasks and responsibilities that affect you as well."

"You can't be serious," Mother snaps. "Her?"

I'm honestly surprised by her outrage. As a woman of great strategic intellect, how could she not have anticipated my intentions? Is she so conceited that she thinks after everything she's put me through—all the bullying and dismissal—that I will choose *her* to sit at my side?

Not in this lifetime or the next.

"You are Father's queen, Mother, not mine. You've had decades to rule. Once I ascend as Fae Prime, Calli will be your queen. You need to come to terms and respect that."

"You ask too much, Nakotah. You have no idea what the station of Prime and Prima involves. The Fae Council and the heads of state and the people who matter in the world beyond expect certain things."

"Isn't that why you've come? To prepare me in person instead of by video conferencing as agreed?"

Between Mother's indignance, Calli swaying against me with her need pulsing, and Keyla and Raven's raised eyebrows, holding a straight face is getting difficult. Still, I am to be king, so I must at least act the part.

With my arm around my mate, I turn us as one and escort her toward the living room. "Come along. Mother. Keyla and I have our computers set up for the meeting in here. You truly needn't have come all this way simply to turn around and fly back in an hour or two."

Mother sputters behind me. "An hour or two? Am I not welcome to stay in your home?"

I offer her what I hope is a respectful smile, though it is a challenge. "Not during our mating alignment, no. Even if you don't respect our feelings on being the chosen quint, the Fae Council placed priority on readying Calli to transform and open the gate to Stone-Haven. That means we need privacy to continue in—how did you put it before you threw me out—our tawdry behavior."

My soul crystal warms against my sternum. I don't know what it means, but it feels to me that it senses the rightness of my commitment to Calli and our mating bonds.

"Come now," I gesture toward the living room again. "Let us finish our business. Our mates will be home in a few hours and I, for one, am looking forward to having the house to ourselves. I'm sure you remember how it was when you and Father first mated. It's an exciting time."

~

*Hawk*

I'm still mulling over Jaxx's 'trust the boundaries' comment when the second team arrives. The SUV eases off the road and pulls in behind ours. Heart-to-heart time is over.

"Okay, let's see what they found out. Shall we?"

My phone rings and I check the caller ID. And just like that, my concentration is blown. "Jaxx, you go ahead, I have to take this."

The jaguar strides off to chat with team two about what they learned at the storage unit and I pull up my big-boy pants and answer my phone. "Jayne. What do you need?"

"Where are you? I sent a courier with the monthly reports to Northwood Hall but was told you weren't the one who signed for them."

"Who did?"

"Maggie Stanton."

"Fine. That's Jaxx's mother. I trust she won't do anything duplicitous with the monthlies. I'll review them when I return. Is there anything else?"

She sighs on the other end of the line and I can picture the disapproving frown that goes along with it. "Whether or not your mother-in-law assumed our paperwork is not the point. We co-run a corporation, darling. I need to know where you are in case something urgent happens. I checked the travel logs and—"

Of course, she did. "You needn't keep tabs on me, Jayne. Things I do outside of the FCO aren't your concern."

"So, your trip to Oregon this morning is personal?"

"Brant has a sleuth matter to attend to in his home territory. We are a package deal now, the five of us."

"Isn't his sleuth's business buffalo ranching?"

"Among other things, yes."

There's a long pause and then she sighs. "Hawk, listen to me, I don't like where our relationship has gone. You're mated now. I accept that. It wasn't something either of us chose, but we are a spectacular team. Don't throw away years of trust and partnership simply because the universe screwed you over."

I blink at the night sky and check my mirrors. Two weeks ago, I would have agreed with her. A lot can happen in two weeks. A lot *has* happened.

"Our estrangement isn't because of my mating, it's because you orchestrated a clusterfuck ambush on Calli. You deliberately misled her and blatantly overstepped to retain a hold on me you never truly possessed."

"How was I to guess she'd devolve into a lunatic?"

I revisit the scene of me tackling Jayne behind the couch as fireballs blazed past my head. It will likely be funny one day but today isn't that day. If I had it to do over again, I wouldn't have saved Jayne. I would've let her fry or at least get singed. "You underestimated her and were intentionally cruel. Plain, and simple."

"And I apologized. What more would you have me do?"

It pisses me off that she thinks a few words can erase the damage done. It pisses me off more that I used those exact words after I broke Calli's barriers down to save Jaxx.

Words are not enough. I shall forever endeavor to make amends for that. "Nothing. There's nothing to be done except for your job. Is there anything else?"

"Only that Hunter asked about your return earlier. I believe he has Operations matters he wants to discuss with you and he, like many, are finding it unsettling that the man at the helm of this corporation hasn't been at the helm for weeks."

I end the call and roll my eyes. "If only there were three of me, maybe I could be everywhere I need to be at once."

# CHAPTER SIX

Brant

*L*ukas and I maneuver the angled sections of the bad guy's rooftop, search the areas around the house we can safely access without tipping anyone off to our presence, and return to our starting position to compare notes.

Taking a knee to keep out of sight, I point a thumb behind me. "On the south side of the mansion, there's a pool house. Windows dark, door locked. By the size of it, there couldn't be more than one bedroom. Definitely not big enough to house fourteen gifted kids. On the east, against the perimeter wall, there's a garden shed about the size of a normal one-car garage."

Lukas dips his chin. "The north gives us a four-car garage similar to the one at the place we're staying. Could be a loft apartment above there. I didn't see any guards, but we don't know anything about our captors. Maybe they've washed or programmed these kids so thoroughly they're not worried about escape."

Damn, I hate thinking about them being mentally manipulated like that. "Can Hawk's man Fiske undo the memory wash he performed?

Is there a chance these kids can go home and everything be like it was?"

Lukas shrugs. "Not my department. By my experience, though, there's never any 'going back' when something as disruptive as this happens. Even if Fiske can undo what was done, the trauma will leave an echo."

"I guess it's too soon to worry about that. First, we've got to find the kids and secure them."

"True enough. We'll start our search in the garage and then move into the main house. There's a service entrance at the back I can work my magic on to gain access. Good to go?"

"Always. I've got your six."

We move out and make our way down to the garage. It's a slow progression because we're taking every precaution not to be discovered by perimeter guards cloaked for invisibility. I'm accustomed to being more of a rush in and split heads FCO Enforcer rather than a covert FCO Investigations Officer but I follow Lukas's lead and we stay hidden.

The garage is a dead end.

The loft above the cars is used as a workout center and does not indicate that anyone stays up there.

We're back outside and accessing the staff entrance to the laundry room when a set of car headlights sweep the lawn. We backflat against the building and I hope there is enough shadow to conceal a man of my size.

The hum of the garage door sends a wave of warm and tinglies crawling over my skin. If they'd arrived five minutes earlier, Lukas and I would've been inside searching for the access point to the loft.

I ease a foot or two away from the entrance to make sure I'm good and hidden.

The *thunk* of two doors precedes the distant convo of two men. By the sound of things, they're worker bees sent for supplies. The garage door hums and descends as our two runners carry their purchases around the front and into the house.

Lukas times the opening of the staff door with the *beep-ba-beep-beep* of the front door chime and we're in.

From here on, it's hand signals and listening. It takes us another fifteen minutes to sweep the house, learn there are five men inside, and sounds of pre-pubescent laughter coming from the third floor.

I text our findings to Hawk and his response comes back immediately. *Sending team two in to secure the house. Position yourselves to secure the kids.*

Finally, we agree. My thinking exactly. I show Lukas the screen of my phone and we're on the move again.

Lukas stops in the stairwell ahead of me and signals for me to hold position. The third floor is lit like Times Square on New Year's. There's no chance of us getting an inch up the hall without being in full view.

Lukas checks his watch and leans against the wall.

I get it. We'll wait until all hell breaks loose downstairs and then make a rush. The only problem with that is we don't know what we're facing until shit hits.

Are there cloaked guards? Are there guards in with the kids? If there *is* a guard in with the teens, we'll be forcing a hostage situation. How many kids are up here? With more questions than answers, we sit tight and bide our time.

*Calli*

Kotah's mom is a conniving bitch. I'd never say that to him but I can think it—and I do. While he and his sister are busy chatting with Raven and taking notes on duties and schedules and who they can depend on for what within the palace hierarchy, Malayna takes advantage of every opportunity to ingratiate herself into what's to come.

He'll need her for this. The Fae Council will expect her to be included in that. According to her take on things, there are too many moving parts for her to be considered dispensable. If Kotah and Keyla are to have any chance at success, they need to sweep the idea of going it alone out of their heads and accept her humble offer to help them.

"I have a question," I say, interrupting her current tangent of self-promo. "What happens when the Northwood term is up? Who's next on the ruling roster?"

"The Highborn Elves of Lorea," Raven answers.

"And how long will Kotah and Keyla be expected to continue their duties after the elves are in power?"

"There is a six-week transition period when the duties are taken over. Three weeks before the elves take power where they have access to you and Nakotah to discuss duties, and then another three weeks after they're sworn in where you two shadow them and offer guidance when required."

"And that's it? Then it's their show?"

Raven nods. "Of course. Each Prime is encouraged to run his time of service how he and his chosen leaders see fit. We have found this timeframe more than adequate for the transition of power in the past."

"Perfect, so then, since Kotah and Keyla are a week into meetings with you and already have such a thorough working knowledge of palace life, there shouldn't be any problem with them seizing the reins of Kotah's rule when the time comes that he's called to step up."

Raven bites her bottom lip and I catch the furtive glance she casts towards her queen. "That is correct."

"Excellent."

"What are you playing at, Calliope?" Malayna says, her glare sending ocular daggers to impale me.

"Only that if each Fae Prime is encouraged to take his rule in his own direction, Kotah deserves the same opportunity. He's incredibly insightful and compassionate. I think he'll raise the bar of an integrated fae existence to new levels once we open the gates to Stone-Haven. It's an exciting time. Maybe that's even part of the reason he was chosen as one of the Guardians of the Phoenix. Maybe his destiny reaches beyond what any past Prime has been asked to do."

I reach forward for my raspberry cooler and regret it. I'd almost gotten accustomed to the vibrator and having Kotah's mother here certainly dampens all moods of pleasure, but the shift in position does me no favors.

By the smirk on Kotah's face, he's read my dilemma. "Here, let me." He hands me my drink and chuckles. "Do you need anything else, *Chigua?*"

*Just your cock hammering inside me while I come apart at the seams.* I take two deep gulps. "No. I'm good."

Raven is gracious enough to restart the discussion and everyone ignores the haughty indignance pluming off Kotah's mother. *Grow the hell up, queenie. You're not all that.*

*Way to go, girlfriend. Sock it to the bitch.*

I startle and search the faces of the others. Did they not hear her? *Riley? Riley, can you hear me?*

I don't realize I've shifted to the edge of my chair until Kotah puts a hand on my thigh. "Calli? Are you well?"

I blink and meet the concerned gaze of Keyla. "You went white as a sheet there."

The Prima makes a tsking sound and frowns. "You'll soon find drama and histrionics don't get you far in the fae court. Even if my son is too hormone-struck to see through you, others will."

I laugh. "Then how have you gotten anything done?"

"Enough," Kotah says, standing. "I've had enough for one day. I'm sorry you both traveled all this way for so little progress. Raven, perhaps next time you'll stick to our agreed plans, or if you need an in-person visit come alone."

By the looks of Raven and Keyla, they strongly agree.

It's Keyla who speaks, though. "Mother, perhaps you and I could step outside and enjoy some evening air while Kotah and Raven finish up. It's a lovely evening and there is a gazebo beyond the waterfall of the pool. Calli, could you take notes for me?"

I accept her notepad and settle back into my seat. "Of course. Enjoy your walk."

*Hawk*

Jaxx and I will load into the backseat for the incursion," I say. Jaxx arches a brow and I shrug. "It's more important for the security team to exit the vehicle quickly and get inside the house. We'll await the all-clear."

He nods and climbs inside. "I didn't realize you knew how to take the backseat for anythin', avian."

I chuckle and climb in to take the seat beside him. Maybe I haven't given Jaxx enough credit. He's actually a funny guy.

"Have I got a greenlight, sir?" Griggs, the team leader of team two asks, meeting my gaze in the rear-view mirror.

"We're a go," I say, gripping the seatback of the middle row with one hand and the holy-shit handle with the other.

The female, Hannah, raises the detonator for the explosives placed on the gate. "Bango in three, two, one."

The gates blow inward with a bang and a wall of smoke. Griggs drops his foot on the gas and we ram past the debris and head toward the main house.

There's nothing stealth about our entry. The moment the explosion goes off, floodlights activate along the perimeter walls and we've likely drawn the attention of everyone inside the house. Hopefully, that includes fourteen exceptional teens.

The truck jolts to a halt at the front door and the team explodes out of the vehicle. Three rush the front door, and the other two split and circle the building in opposite directions.

"Well, that was exciting," Jaxx says, releasing his hold. "As EMS, I never get to be part of the action. This is fun."

We exit the truck and I draw my Sig. Scanning sightlines while moving to the back of the truck, I ensure nobody has a direct line of sight to either of us. "I've got a full med-kit back here for you, should you need it."

Jaxx joins me and while he's looking through the offerings, I monitor the sightlines and watch his back. He may be a gifted paramedic, but he has no tactical instinct.

I make a mental note to add that to the daily training sessions. Thus far, we've been so focused on bringing Calli up to speed, we haven't gotten familiar with the skills and attributes of the guardians.

That was an oversight that needs to be rectified.

We can all fight, I have no doubts about that. Our wildling sides and aggression levels weigh in heavily on that front. What we need to do is hone tactical awareness.

*Bang. Bang.*

Two shots go off inside and Jaxx stiffens and grabs the kit. "That can't be good."

I gesture for him to round the truck so we're standing with the vehicle between us and any hostile force exiting the house on a run. "Take this. Do you remember how to shoot?"

All FCO officers, no matter what their position, are taught basic offense and defense before being allowed to work in the field.

Jaxx sets the medical bag on the ground between his feet and accepts the gun. "*Remember?* Silly, Hawk. Did you forget I'm from Texas?"

"Not everyone in Texas is raised with a gun in his hand."

"Everyone I know was. In my circles, gun control means buying one when you really want two."

A clamor at the front of the house has Brant tackling a runner down three stone steps. Jaxx and I are coming around the hood of the truck when a teenaged girl does a flying dive off the top step and wraps herself around our bear.

"Shit. Is that one of the kids we're saving?"

"Looks like it."

Brant realizes that as well because he's fighting with his opponent while making no attempt to dislodge the banshee starfish beating on him from behind.

I fire a warning shot into the night sky and it's enough to get the girl's attention. Brant takes advantage of her distraction and shucks her off into a hedge.

The guy he's fighting breaks free and flees down the driveway like he's been shot out of a rocket. Brant takes chase and I fall in behind him as backup.

"Jaxx, you've got the girl."

# CHAPTER SEVEN

## Kotah

*O*nce Keyla escorts Mother outside, the toxicity levels in the air drop way down. It never ceases to amaze me how one tiny woman can contaminate and monopolize every situation. If there was an Olympics for personal and political manipulation, my mother would clean up the medals.

"I'm so sorry," Raven says, offering us both a sincere apology. "I had every intention of joining you in a video chat. Somehow your mother found out we had a meeting scheduled and here we are."

I wave her concern away. "Not for one minute, did I think any of this is your fault."

I get up to stretch my legs and stroll over to the glass patio doors. Mother and my sister are headed out toward the gazebo. Good. A little distance will do all of us some good.

How Keyla can stand to spend time alone with her I shall never truly understand. It speaks to my sister's character that she has the strength to deal with her without devolving into manipulation herself.

"I'm well aware of my mother's tricks. I don't hold you responsible for her sudden appearance in our lives. She doesn't appreciate losing her hold on me. It's only going to get worse as my position solidifies."

Raven nods and offers Calli an appraising smile. "That bit about the elves and the time of transition was brilliant. Well played. It's not every day that someone hits a home run against the Prima."

Calli shrugs, tipping back her cooler and finishing it. "I've survived worse than her. Not growing up in your world, I hold no awe for the pomp of her title. Maybe that helps me see her solely for the woman she is. How someone so petty and vicious could have raised a son so tender and thoughtful is the thing of awe from where I stand."

I lean over the back of her chair to kiss the top of her head. "Ever my dauntless defender."

She reaches back and pats my fingers on her shoulder. "You better believe it. You decide who you want in your court and how that's going to look. No one else."

A scream in the back yard has me rushing to the patio door. I yank back the glass slab and bolt through the doorway. Doc and I launch off the back deck at the same time, hitting the lawn at a run.

My sister is surrounded, as men in black seeth from the shadows and she stands between them and my mother.

"Keyla!"

*Brant*

Damn this asshole's got legs. I pump my arms and beat feet as fast as my tactical boots can carry me. The thundering *thump-thump-thump* of my long stride isn't getting me any closer to catching up. My bear growls as my thigh muscles burn and my lungs begin to catch fire. I'm not sure how long I can keep up in a flat-out run behind this guy.

I've got my sights locked on the runner, so it's a jarring shock when I get clotheslined and taken to ground—by nothing. I suppose *no one* would be more accurate.

Well. At least no one I could see.

Dammit. The cloaked guards.

One connects a lucky kick to my ribs, but I grab at the hit and grip his foot. Invisible or not, I twist until it snaps. The scream tells me right where his face is, and I grapple up his body and clock him with a right hook.

I'm not sure if there are more, but I don't have time to worry about it. Back on my feet, I'm launching off again when Hawk goes flying past me in pursuit.

*Shit*, where did he come from?

I watch my footing as I dodge what is left of the front gate, and we bank a hard right. He's trying to lose us, ducking down side streets and weaving his way in and out of shadows.

A few blocks away from the mansion, he takes an alley edged by rusted out old cars, dumpsters, and empty lots. This guy is moving too damned fast to be human.

Doesn't matter. If he leads us to our Black Knight it doesn't matter what he is or where he thinks he's going.

He's ours.

Hawk is hot on his heels, gaining a few inches with every stride. Damn, the avian can run too. Makes sense,

As dense as my bones and muscles are because I'm a bear—Hawk's a bird. He's got to have less mass to make his transitions into his hawk form and fly.

I'm twenty or thirty feet behind them and losing ground. Neither of them seems to be having trouble with the rough and uneven side-walk, but I'm still a bit wonky from my scrap with the invisible man and it trips me up. I almost tumble head over heels at a patch of broken concrete but manage to save my stride.

I can't do anything about the momentum I lose.

Our man drops out of sight down a narrow dirt track between a pair of industrial-looking buildings that speak of better days. When Hawk disappears around the corner, too, I pull an extra burst of power from my bear's strength.

At the same time, I try to access my bond with the others.

We need backup and it would help if someone knows where to

find us. I round the corner and see Hawk closing in on the guy—too quickly.

With how fast he was booking it, there's no way he's running out of gas like that. No. He's deliberately slowing his pace. Hawk doesn't seem to connect the dots. He's focused on the chase—too focused.

"Hawk, stop!" I can't tell if he hears me or not but he doesn't slow. I know how strong the call of the hunt is when I'm locked on a target and I'm a beta.

Hawk is all alpha.

The guy turns and another shot cracks off in the night. Hawk's rhythm is lost as he twists and dodges to the side, but he doesn't slow.

Our bad guy's non-human status is sealed when he takes a ten-foot fence at a running leap.

Hawk launches into the air, gets his hands over the top edge, and pulls himself up and over.

Another two shots.

Shit. I can't see what's on the other side of the fence.

I repeat Hawk's performance and take a flying leap to grab the top edge of the fence and flip over onto the other side. I'm still in freefall on the opposite side when the metal tang of blood hits me.

It's heavy in the air and I soon see why.

Hawk is down and bleeding bad.

A guttural growl has me searching the darkness. Two sets of golden eyes shift forward from the shadows of the gated yard. Two Rottweilers, heads down and teeth bared.

"Well, fuck."

*Calli*

Keyla's scream sends shards of ice through my guts. I chase Kotah out the back door and am right on his heels as he bounds down the stairs of the back deck. The sounds of fists to flesh hang in the still night air.

The shadows are writhing with men throwing punches near the gazebo.

Someone is dragging Keyla across the lawn toward the gate. Doc, Keyla's two guards, and the Prima's palace guards are there but overwhelmed by attackers. Kotah's growl is more menacing than I've ever heard it. The fury of being attacked in our place of privacy burns in my blood too.

My phoenix ignites within.

My skin starts to glow gold as—

A blue bolt of icy energy hits me in the shoulder and knocks me spinning into the pool. I hit the water with a backward momentum that swamps me in seconds. Salt burns my nostrils and my throat as I kick back to the surface.

So. Rude.

"I'm fine," I sputter, sensing more than seeing Kotah's conflict of saving me or his sister. The water steams around my face as I flame out. "Help Keyla."

I told Jaxx this afternoon that I wanted to take a swim tonight. This isn't what I had in mind. A quick breaststroke takes me to the ladder, and I haul myself out. My clothes hang heavy and feel gross, but there's no time to worry about that.

My soggy socks are barely on the marble slab of the pool deck when I've got incoming. What the hell.

Give a girl a second to catch her breath.

Do I want the pool at my back so no one gets behind me or do I want to avoid getting dunked and drowned? I don't know which would be better. I try to call on my phoenix but whatever that icy energy pulse was that took me into the pool is chilling my fiery side down.

I dodge the incoming right cross and settle in for the fight. One guy is swinging, another is trying to grab me, the third has a gun but he's screened by the other two.

This I know how to deal with.

If nothing else, over the past two weeks, the guys have been drilling in melee fighting skills. I'm getting pretty confident in hand to hand... even without my orange spatula of raging fire.

Gun guy is trying to get around the others but is having trouble because the pool is at my back. Okay, I'll pretend I meant to do that. Yay me.

I'm swatting away grabby guy when punchy guy lands a solid shot to my jaw. My head pivots with the force of the blow and I honestly see stars. The light show has me blinking, but I don't drop my guard. He might have rung my bell, but he isn't going to win the fight.

The *chuff-chuff-chuff* of rotor blades has me glaring at the helicopter landing on the back lawn. Damn. These guys are serious. I try to call on my flames again, but whatever chill I caught, it's still holding on.

Dammit.

I see the Taser pointed at me too late. The high-pitched whine of a power-up draws my attention just as the probes shoot into my boob. I stiffen as fifty-thousand volts of raw energy short out my brain.

Punchy moves in and places an acrid-sweet cloth over my face. The world and my will to fight drift away.

◈

*Jaxx*

I finish patching up the downstairs guard's bullet wound and hand him off to the FCO officers to do with him what they will. "He'll be fine. It's a clean shot through the meat of his shoulder. It didn't impact anythin' vital. It'll also be a great place to apply pressure if the interrogation isn't goin' well."

"Fuck you, feline," the guy sputters.

"Yeah, you're welcome." I smile and move back to my first patient to see how he's healing up. "Hey, Lukas. How you feelin' now, my man?"

"Pissed and ready to kill someone."

I stop in front of where Hawk's badass, right-hand man is sitting on the third step and check his eyes. His pupils are equal and reactive. His color is back as well. "Well, I'm sure you'll get your chance soon. You're good to go."

Hannah comes jogging down the stairs and Lukas pushes up to his feet and out of her way. "Everyone upstairs seems fine—physically at least. They're confused though."

"So, we got the kids?"

"One cell," Hannah says. "From what we've pieced together, this Black Knight of yours is keeping them split up while he trains and reprograms them. Likely three cells of four kids per cell. We've got the first four upstairs."

"And the banshee girl who attacked Hawk?"

"Upstairs with the others and very confused. She swears she lives here and we're home invaders."

I sigh. "Only four. I can't say I'm not disappointed."

"Hey, once we get some help to them, it'll be a solid win for these four." Hannah's gaze shifts to Lukas next. "I've been trying to get our next steps from Mr. Barron. He mentioned taking the kids to the compound he rented and putting them in a garage loft? I haven't gotten confirmation on that. Do either of you know where we go from here?"

Lukas taps the comm in his ear and it beeps to life. "Sir, we got four of the kids. Where do we go from here?" The guy waits for a bit and then frowns. "Hawk? You hearing me? Hawk, check-in. Where are you?"

His pinched brow raises my hackles. "He and Brant went off after a runner. Here, I'll try calling them." I pull up Hawk's number first and it goes to voicemail. I call Brant's next and get the same thing. "Okay, I'm hating this."

Lukas frowns and starts tapping his phone. After a few seconds, a map fills the screen and a blue dot appears. "Grab your med-kit, Jaguar. I've got him. Let's roll."

I grab my gear and am hot on Lukas's heels as we hustle back to the SUV. The doors are still open from the mass exodus of the incursion team, so we slam those shut and close the tailgate before we get going.

Lukas hands me his phone and gets us moving. I study the screen as it recalibrates and start the navigation. "Out of the gate, take a right. Two blocks up, a left."

It goes like that, the side streets and alleyways passing in a blur as I close in on Hawk's location. When the SUV jolts to a stop, we're staring at the ten-foot security fence of what seems to be a testing facility of some kind.

"I'll take a look." Being a jaguar has advantages even when I'm in human form. I set down the medical bag and scale the fence with one vaulting leap. Grabbing the top edge of the fence, I peer over the top and try to take it in.

The carnage. The blood.

"Brant? Is that you?"

The giant grizzly bear turns his head and lets off a throaty bellow.

"Yeah, I'm glad to see you too, buddy." With my mouth open to speak, the scent receptors in my tongue sort through the different sources of blood. Some canine, some Brant's, but a huge percentage of it is Hawk's. I drop my gaze to the heap of male right below me at the base of the fence. "Oh shit. Okay, hang on. Help is here."

"Thank fuck!" Brant says flipping to two feet from four.

I drop off the fence and frown. "Lukas, if it's in your power, I need this fence gone. Hawk's wedged against the bottom on the other side and circling the drain."

A second later, there's no fence. Lukas stands, hands poised, and magic snapping in the air.

"Now that's cheating," Brant says, dropping to his knee on the asphalt. "We got pinned down by guard dogs and he was in no shape to get back over the fence. Thanks for tracking us down."

Even with the night vision of my jaguar, I can't see shit with all the blood getting in the way. "Get him flat on his back and strip off his shirt."

The two of them lay Hawk out and do as I asked while I dig into the bag for the tourniquet. "He's lost a lot of blood. Brant, do you have doctors in any local hospitals that we can trust to get us a wildling top up?"

Brant frowns. "Not close enough to be of any use. Doc's our best bet. He's got mad skills."

My hands are slick, and I'm fumbling to tie off the pressure band. I do a quick check for other injuries, but I can't see shit. "Okay, good enough. Let's move."

"I'll call Calli and get our phoenix girl wound up and ready to help."

"Even with her tears, we'll need blood. I don't suppose the FCO has a blood bank or lab in the neighborhood?"

"I've got him there," Lukas says. "I've topped him up before in a crunch."

"What? Human mage to hawk wildling? That's insane."

Brant scoops Hawk up as if he weighs little more than a kid. "I'm with Jaxx. That's a recipe for disaster."

"I never said it was ideal," Lukas says, jogging ahead to open the door of the hatch. "After a bit of a battle, his body will accept it."

I wipe my hands on my jeans as we move. "I'm not sure his body can take any more battle than he's already waging."

"It'll work," Lukas snaps.

Brant reaches into the back of the truck and lays Hawk down. "That's where he gets the magic boost."

*Right.* We've speculated about that. Still, knowing how inter-species blood donation works, mage blood should kill him not save him.

I climb in the hatch with Hawk and drop the back seats to give us more room. Still, it's crowded. "Hey, Hawk. Hang in there, my man. We'll get you sorted out as soon as possible. Brant, you're calling Calli, yeah?"

"Yeah," he says, shutting his door. "On it now."

# CHAPTER EIGHT

## Calli

*I* rouse with the fumes of car exhaust in my nose and a pounding throb in my head. By the constant whir and bump as we move along, I guess that I'm in the trunk of a car. My first instinct is to flame out, heat the gas tank, and blow these fuckers to bits. But I don't know where Kotah and Keyla are. If they're in the car too, Keyla wouldn't survive. Kotah might... the guys don't seem to suffer from my fire now that we're mated. Still, it's too risky.

I shift to ease the pain in my right shoulder where something metal is poking me. My arms are tied behind my back, but that's the work of a moment. As pissed as I am, that plastic cable tie has no choice but to melt away.

Rubbing the tender flesh around my wrists, I soothe the pinched skin. Okay, recap. We were attacked in the back yard... I was tasered and drugged... helicoptered somewhere... and now on a road trip.

My life is one big adventure.

I press a hand to my chest and frown at the emotions I'm getting from my mates. Closing my eyes, I focus on where the pain is coming from. They're all distraught. Hawk's hurt.

I feel him slipping from our bond and I focus on strengthening our hold on him. What's happening? Where are they? Where am I?

The answer comes back to me with a moment of dawning clarity. I have no idea where I am, but I know that none of my mates are anywhere near me. And if I'm not near Hawk, I can't help him.

I also know, without a doubt, Kotah's not in the car.

What about Keyla?

Shifting around to the back of the seat, I fumble in the dark for the seat release. Carefully, I pull the release and ease the seat forward enough to see that the back seat is empty.

"… a right bad idea."

"That's not for you to decide. In ten minutes, we'll hand her over and be done with the whole thing."

"And yer sure she's out?"

"Yeah, she'll be out another hour at least."

*Wrong, asshole.* Phoenix blood has healing abilities you forgot to take into account. Sucks to be you two. With that, I invite my phoenix to come out and play. My skin burns hot and glows with the fire of my fury igniting within. With both my hands on the floor of the trunk, I focus my fiery intentions toward the gas tank.

The car explodes into a mass of mangled metal and flying shrapnel. Those two thought they could take me from my mates? Fuck that.

Whoever decided this was a good idea doesn't begin to understand how bad things are going to go for them.

I straighten inside the heat of the inferno and my cells suck up the intensity of the explosion. It's a freaking power boost. I raise my arms and my wings unfurl. My wingspan reaches across the entire width of the two-lane road and it's an awesome sight, even for me.

Each time I connect with my phoenix, she gains strength.

I know what I am and embrace my wildling side.

I connect with Hawk's suffering and push from the ground. My mate needs me. My wings pump against the darkness of the night sky forcing the cool night air downward as I climb. I'm doing it. I'm flying.

For two incredible minutes, I gain altitude and distance from those

who conspire to hurt me. Then I flame out and fall from the sky...
"Oh shit."

*Brant*

"What the fuck do you mean, she was taken?" My voice is laced with
all the fury and frustration of my night. Only getting four kids free,
Hawk getting shot, me playing the part of a chew toy for hostile dogs,
and now—worse than all of it combined— "Calli's missing?"

Kotah is barely holding it together, but I haven't got the energy to
care. He was on guardian duty for our mate. "And where the hell were
you when she was getting stuffed into a helicopter?"

"I'm sorry," he says, gutted. "I failed her."

"Bullshit," Keyla says, storming between us. "You need to back your
bear ass down, furball. You weren't here. You have no right to
weigh in."

"She's right," Jaxx says, rounding the corner of the living room.
"Get your head in the game, Bear. While Doc, Lukas, and I are tryin'
to save Hawk's life. You need to track the security footage and figure
out who the fuck took her and where they might've gone."

Jaxx's voice is rarely laced with the command of an alpha, but it is
now, and my bear responds instinctively even if the man is out of his
mind. "I'm on it."

"I'll help," Hannah says, rushing to keep up.

"I don't need your help," I shout.

"Yes, you do, B," she says, frowning as I turn on her. "I'm a skilled
IO and I know this area at least as well if not better than you. Stop
wasting time. Get your ass in there and call up the feeds we need to
review. Two sets of eyes will get through it twice as fast."

My bear lets off a house-shaking roar, but I do what she says and
head into the office.

Hannah's right. She's one helluva keen investigating officer and in
less than five minutes we've got the battle up and running for review.

Going through and highlighting key frames, we get the make and model of the helicopter, and identify three men using the FCO face recognition software she has access to.

"Pull up their profiles," I bark. "Let's find out who these guys are working for."

Kotah's scent is building from out in the hall and I curse. "Come in, buddy. I'm sorry."

Our wolf rounds the corner and my bear writhes inside me at the sight of his glassy eyes and battered body. I've seen the footage. I know the beating he took. I shouldn't have needed to see it in video replay to know he fought with every breath he had to keep her safe.

He'd taken out three and freed his sister before racing back to take on the ones attacking Calli. He'd done his best against insurmountable numbers. I hit my chest with my fist and clear my throat.

"I'm not mad at you, buddy—I'm mad at me. We should've been here. I led Jaxx and Hawk away from you guys because my priorities haven't been the five of us. This is on me. I'm sorry."

I hold out my arms and he doesn't hesitate.

"I swear I tried…"

I bend my head and press my cheek against his head. Breathing in the acrid scent of his anguish I'm reminded that no matter how much we lean on him, in reality, he's still a kid. He's a twenty-year-old student who's lived a life of privilege. Yes, he's had emotional hardship, but that's not the same as the physical scars life hands you over the years.

I ease back, press my lips to his forehead, and brush his tears with my thumbs. "Not your fault. Let's get her back."

He licks his lips and swallows. "How do we do that?"

"We figure out who took her and what they want. Are they part of a Darkside plot? Are they with the Black Knight? Are the two the same thing? Are they—"

"—all employed by the royal palace," Hannah says, straightening.

"What?"

She gestures to the screen. The photos and profiles of five of the men have now been matched and their information was gathered as part of their security screening to work for palace security. "Who at the Prime Palace would want Calli kidnapped and taken by force."

Kotah goes deathly still and a furious roar rips from his throat. He turns and between the desk and the door, he's flipped into his wolf form and is gunning it on four feet back to the living room.

"Oh fuck!" I vault over the desk my boots squeaking on the floor as I chase behind him. "Kotah, wait."

But there's no reasoning with him. His wolf has taken over and the man is lost to his fury. The screaming in the living room tells me I'm too late. I round the corner and Kotah has his mother pinned to the area rug, his teeth closed around her throat.

"Kotah, stop!" Keyla shouts. "What's wrong with you? What happened?"

"Everyone back off," I shout, pointing to the two royal guards conflicted on whether they should be protecting their Prima or respecting the Prime in Waiting. No one is moving, so I try it again with feeling. "Back the fuck off!"

Raven tugs at Keyla and the guards back away. I kneel on the rug next to Kotah and make sure he can see me. "Easy, buddy. As much as I know you want to rip her throat out, we don't have all the facts here."

"All the facts about what?" Keyla shouts. "What's gotten into him? He's never violent."

"He's never had his mate targeted and taken from him." I reach to stroke the stunning chocolate and silver coat of my mate. His shoulders tense and his mother whimpers beneath the clasp of his teeth. "Easy buddy. If you kill her, you'll regret it later. I know you will and somewhere in there, you know it too."

"Kill her?" Keyla snaps. "Why would he want to kill her? She torments him, yes. I know he holds no affection for her, but he's never wished to do her harm."

"The men who attacked you were all registered as palace guards," I say, keeping my voice calm and my tone even. "They didn't make any move on your mother, did they? No. Because an assault on the Prima is grounds for death. They targeted you and dragged you away so Kotah would be focused on you instead of Calli."

"No," Keyla says, shaking her head. "There has to be a mistake. Mother's manipulative and heartless but she's not stupid. She knows Calli's the phoenix. She's the harbinger of unity for the realms."

"Your parents don't want the realms united," Raven says, her hand at her throat. "I overheard them talking about how there are so many unknowns in opening the portal it could destabilize this realm and weaken their position as rulers."

Kotah's growl grows louder and tears fall down the Prima's cheek. She's attempting to talk but she can't. Kotah's hold on her throat is preventing all movement.

"Let her live, my man," I say, trying again to touch him. This time he doesn't threaten to crush the Prima's windpipe, so I take that as consent. I run my fingers into his long, luscious coat and try to connect with the man inside. "She might have answers we need to finding Calli. She's our best lead in discovering who has here and where they took her. C'mon, Wolf. You have to let her go, if only for Calli's sake."

*Kotah*

I hear the wisdom in Brant's words, but it's a struggle to force my wolf to comply. With everything in me, I want my mother to pay for her part in whatever Calli is suffering right now. It doesn't surprise me that my parents would conspire against me to keep the portal gate closed.

It *does* surprise me how much it still hurts.

"Kotah," Keyla says, kneeling beside me opposite Brant. "Please, big brother. Let her go. We'll find out who did what. Focus on getting your mate back as quickly as we can. Calli needs you to be thoughtful here not reactive."

I hear the tears in my sister's voice and I'm sorry for putting them there, but she's wrong. I already know who is behind this abduction as firmly as I know that the bitch will deny it until her dying day.

But she's also right. Finding Calli is my priority. With one last growl, I roll off my mother and shift back. I'm on my feet and pacing in my next breath, putting distance between me and the woman I could kill without a second thought.

"Why Mother?" I ask rebounding. "Are you angry that she means everything to me? Do you really fear becoming irrelevant so badly that you'd condemn the people two realms their access to family and loved ones? Or are you simply such a fucking bitch that you can't stand to lose my compliance?"

Keyla and Raven help her onto the couch and she juts her chin. "How can you believe these lies, Nakotah? I am your mother. I gave birth to you. I raised you from a pup and nurtured you—"

"No, you didn't. You belittled me and left me for others to deal with. We both know you and father never gave two shits about me. It was Naquilla you wanted, the boy who should've been prime. He's dead, Mother, and I'm an Omega. Every time I disappointed you, I felt how much you wished I died instead of him."

"That's not tru—"

"Sure, it is," I say, throwing up my hands. "I can't help what I was born and won't apologize for it. I stopped caring what you and Father say long before I was chosen as one of the Guardians of the Phoenix."

"Nakotah, I don't know what's gotten into—"

"Save the moral indignation, Prima. It wasn't Calli who turned me against you and Father. It was you and Father. Now, the only thing you're good for is telling us who has her and where they've taken her."

"I told you, I have no idea."

"And I know it's pointless to appeal to your better nature because you haven't got one. Get out of this house and out of my life. I hope to never see you again. In fact, make it your life's mission to avoid me because the next time I do, Brant might not be around to talk me down."

"Stop this impudence!" she shouts. "I am your mother and I'm telling you—"

I flip back into my wolf and advance with my jaws snapping and my growl wild. She flinches and rushes to her feet. Raven guides her past the coffee table and into the care of her two royal guards. Keyla rushes to see them out.

I shift back to human form and don't let my knees unlock until the latch of the door clicks shut and I'm more confident I won't chase after her and rip her to shreds.

"Kotah," Keyla says. "Do you honestly think she did this to you... and to Calli?"

"I do. She knew where we were when none of us told her or anyone else. The men were all part of her staff. She and Father don't want the portal gate opened... yes, I think she did this. I'm sorry. I know you try to maintain a relationship with her, but I'm done with both of them."

Brant squeezes my shoulder and gives me a sad nod. "Come, Wolf. Let's get to work and find our mate."

# CHAPTER NINE

Calli

*T*alk about crash and burn. The wind whistles in my ears as I plummet to the ground. My magical flight extinguished almost as soon as I gained momentum but I'm still a couple of hundred feet off the ground. The pain of my body breaking on impact is indescribable. I blackout after I hit hard and plow the earth into a trench. With a throaty *whoosh*, everything around me goes up in flame and I'm engulfed. I close my eyes, too lost to care.

Each time I wake up, I feel a little closer to being alive.

My phoenix healing ability is incredible.

By the third...or maybe it's the fourth trip back to consciousness, it's morning. I hear the voices of men in the distance and roll to my knees to take a look over the lip of the trench I made in the earth.

Have my kidnappers found me?

I breathe a sigh of relief to see the red truck and a small fire response team. They're taking in the smoking char of what would've been some poor farmer's fall crop.

*Oops*, my bad.

When their attention shifts to another section of the field, I stand, check my footing, and make my way toward the firetruck. I manage to get all but the last thirty feet before they notice me and their eyes flare wide.

"Any chance I can get a fire blanket to cover up?" I say, covering my essentials the best I can.

One of the firemen jogs to the engine and grabs one from a compartment inside the truck. He rushes over and holds the blanket up for me to wrap myself inside. "Are you okay? What happened? Where'd you come from?"

I let the weight of the blanket over my shoulders ground me and try to think of a reasonable answer. "I, uh… I was in a car explosion last night and woke up here."

"What happened to your clothes?"

"They caught fire."

"See," the farmer said, "I told you there's a connection. Maybe she shucked her clothes off in my wheat and started the fire. It's not an act of god, it's vandalism."

The man in charge is wearing a white shirt and driving a fire chief truck. He offers the farmer a patient smile and shakes his head. "Mr. Moke. I don't see how discarded clothing could burn hot enough to do this kind of damage. By the time she got from the explosion site to here, they would've been burned off. Don't worry, we'll investigate."

"But I need this crop, Chief. The insurance company won't cover my costs if I can't prove—"

"Don't panic, Mr. Moke," I say, butting into the conversation. "I'll have someone from my husband's company come out to assess the damage. You don't need to make a claim. I'll make sure he covers the market value of what the crop was worth to you. I'm sorry for any trouble this caused."

The farmer narrows his gaze and frowns. "Yeah? You sayin' you did it?"

"Not intentionally, no. But with the explosion and the fire, you're right to think it might be connected. My husband will settle up. Don't you worry."

Now it's the fire chief's turn to eye me up. "That's quite an offer, miss. And who is your husband?"

"His name is Hawk Barrons."

There's a dawning of understanding I wasn't expecting and the chief nods. "That would make you Calliope, yes?"

I take a step back assessing my routes of escape.

The chief raises his palms and waves off my panic. "You're in friendly company, Calli. I'm Grant Davies. I believe we have a friend in common, Brant Robbins. Big fellow, bit of a bear at times. He's my kin."

I let off a gasp of relief. "Yes. Can you call him and tell him where we are? I don't know where I am, and my phone burned up in the explosion."

~

*Hawk*

My rise to consciousness is neither pleasant nor quick. Maybe it's the drugs dripping into my arm via the IV or maybe it's the mental quick-sand I'm fighting not to be swallowed up. Either way, something about my situation doesn't sit right. If only I had the mental juice to figure out what it is.

"Hey," Doc says, from his seat in the corner. "Glad to see you awake. Can I get you anything?"

"What happened?"

"You caught two bullets during your chase down. When Jaxx and Lukas found you and Brant, you were taking your final bow."

"Brant's all right?"

"Perfectly healthy. I had to wrap his forearms for the damage done by two guard dogs, but he's all healed up now."

I remember disjointed flashes of Brant fighting off something and him cursing quite spectacularly while doing it. "Did we get the kids?"

"Four. Hannah and her team are investigating the theory that they've been divided into cells and are being held in different places along the Pacific Coast. Last I heard, she thought she found a potential link to a small town in Northern California. Lukas is with her now helping with the questioning and going through the statements of the teens."

I swallow and reach for the edge of the sheets. Doc is on his feet and jogging over in the next breath. "Not yet, Hawk. Give it another hour or two. I almost didn't get you back and I'd hate to see you waste my efforts by dying now."

"I appreciate the concern, but—" It strikes me then, the something that's not right. "Why am I healing normally? I would've thought Calli would heal me. She healed Jaxx and Brant when they were both near death."

Doc's expression tightens. "Women, right? You can never predict what's going to happen."

Only… *I can.* "Calli is fiercely protective of us. She wants the five of us to work. There's no way…" I toss back the sheets and swing my feet to the floor. "What's wrong? Where is she?"

The rush of blood leaving my head collides with my rising adrenaline and I have to brace my palm against the mattress to keep from keeling over.

"That's what I'm talking about," Doc says, moving to steady me.

I push him back and snap my teeth at him. "My mate! Tell me now."

"I've got this," Jaxx says, striding in. He takes one look at me and frowns. "Thanks, Doc. Seriously, I've got him."

Doc shuffles out of the room like his ass is on fire and my hawk screams a shrill cry in my head. "Where is she? What's wrong?"

Jaxx grabs a t-shirt and a pair of nylon jogging pants off the dresser and brings them back. "I'm going to tell you and you're going to remain as calm as you can manage so Doc lets you leave this room, yeah?"

"I'm not feeling calm, Jaguar."

"I feel you." He grabs a cotton swab off the end table and presses it over the needle puncture as he frees me from the IV. "While we were busy with the raid, a force of more than twenty men invaded the compound and attacked. Calli was taken."

"How the fuck did a hostile force find us?"

"We're still working on that." Jaxx grabs the t-shirt and helps me get it on. The bullet wound in my chest makes lifting my left arm very uncomfortable, but I ignore the pain. "Our location wasn't a complete secret because a couple of hours before the attack, the Prima showed up with Raven and a small entourage. Somehow they found us and thought it would be a nice afternoon for a housecall."

"Fuck. Was the Prima taken too?"

"No. Calli was definitely the target. They left the Prima and targeted Keyla, splitting Kotah's attention. Calli insisted he help his sister and while he fought his way through her attackers, Calli was Tasered and tossed in a helicopter."

He shakes out the pants and holds them open, easing my feet in them one at a time. He leaves them at my knees and starts back at the bottom again with socks and shoes. The alpha in me despises the show of weakness but the mated bond soothes my rage enough to accept the help. "Why aren't you more upset? What do you know?"

"Brant and Kotah found an internet news story about a car explosion further up the coastline near Seattle. Reports describe a fiery burst in the night sky that seemed to launch from the explosion and crash shortly after."

"And?"

"And the field that caught fire was four miles away. Too far for debris to travel."

"You think Calli escaped and got air?"

Jaxx reaches around my back to helps me to my feet. Normally, I'd front and pull away to stand on my own. This morning, I take Jaxx at his word and trust in our bond as mates. I give him my weight, thankful for the support.

"Yeah, that's our working theory. Brant and Kotah are on the road. We're supposed to catch up once you're vertical. Lukas had the helicopter brought over. It's on the back lawn and ready to roll. Shall we?"

## Brant

"Welcome to my old stomping grounds," I say, gesturing to the front windshield in front of us. "I was found in a forest in Washington State as a cub and placed with a sleuth here. It was an amazing place to grow up."

Kotah nods. "It's beautiful."

The kid's been too quiet. Between losing Calli, my reaction, the fight with his mother, and feeling that all of it is his fault, he's barely spoken two words in the past eight hours.

"We'll find her, buddy. You can feel her, right?"

He places his hand on his chest and nods. "Yes. She's doing much better now than she was earlier. Last night, she was in such excruciating pain."

"If we're right about her phoenix taking flight, then we're right about her crashing. She's a phoenix though. The healing is miraculous."

"Still, if she was home with us, she wouldn't have had to suffer alone. She likely wouldn't have crashed at all. I would never have allowed her to get too high on her first flight."

"Things with Calli, are rarely about what we would allow her to do, Wolf. That female has a mind of her own and is tough as rocks."

He nods but doesn't seem any less upset.

My cell rings and the car's Bluetooth connection puts it on the console screen. Grant Davies. I hit accept and keep my eyes on the road. "Hey, Grant. It's not a great time. What can I do for you?"

The chuckle on the other end of the phone. "It's what I can do for you, Bear. Did you lose something precious? Or maybe someone?"

I stare at the display as my heart races. "Do you have her?"

"Safe and sound. She's having a shower here at the station. I'll take her to the ranch when she's ready if that works for you."

"No need," I say, pressing my foot to the floor. "I'm twenty minutes out and coming fast. "Don't let her out of your sight, Grant. There are some real bad people out to get her and she's not ready to face the world alone just yet."

"I've got her, Bear. Just be aware that she's burned off her clothes. Don't rip my throat out because she's wearing a fire blanket."

I chuckle. "Trust me. We're very accustomed to that scenario. We'll be right there. And Grant... thank you. You have no idea how happy you've made us."

I end the call and reach over to take Kotah's hand in mine. I squeeze it and meet the kid's gaze. "See, Wolf. Everything's going to be fine."

~

*Jaxx*

I get Hawk loaded into the helicopter and have him lay on the back bench. He may be upright but it's only by the strength of his will. To say that Doc is pissed is beyond an understatement. Hey, I've been where Hawk is and know the panic of he's feeling. Calli missing and me not well enough to help. Hawk took me to Calli instead of leaving me behind when I was down and out.

I'm returning the favor.

Lukas hands me the med-kit and I set it and our go-bags into the overhead bin. The two of us buckle into the leather captain's chairs facing Hawk and we're ready to roll.

A text rings in and I pull my phone out to read it. "It's Kotah," I say, my smile breaking free as I read the text. "Calli's safe and in the hands of one of Brant's sleuth-mates. They're fifteen minutes from where she is and will update us when they have her. He also sent an address of where to meet them when we come."

Hawk nods. "Lukas... if you will."

Lukas takes my phone and climbs forward to the cockpit of the helicopter.

I stretch my legs and close my eyes. "Rest up, Hawk. We both could use some more sleep. All is well."

"For the moment, anyway."

# CHAPTER TEN

Calli

*I*'m watching out the open door of the engine bay when Brant pulls into the parking lot, shut things down, and bails out almost as quickly as Kotah does. I don't care if I'm supposed to be some majestic mythological wildling, I let off a squeal and run to my men. I'm still wrapped in the fire blanket, so when I open my arms for them, I'm also flashing them the full monty.

They don't seem to mind.

Kotah grabs me up in his arms and Brant wraps himself around us both. "Fuck, it's good to hold you, beautiful."

"It's good to be held."

"I'm so sorry, *Chigua—*"

I squeeze tighter. "Nothing to be sorry about. We were outgunned and outmanned. Not your fault. I'm fine. How's Hawk? I felt his injuries."

"Doc and Jaxx got him patched up. It'll take him some time to recover, but Lukas donated blood and says the magic in his cells will bring him back to full health in a day or two."

"I'm so sorry I wasn't there for him."

"You had no choice in the matter."

"You got air, didn't you?" Brant asks, excitement sparkling in his gold eyes.

"For a few minutes, yeah." I was so angry about the invasion of our compound and worried about Hawk. I wanted to get away from there so badly and needed to get back to you guys… It happened sorta on its own."

"You've been so close," Kotah says, before pressing his lips to my cheek and breathing me in. "I'm proud of you."

"We both are," Brant says, pressing his cheek to the top of my head. "How about we get somewhere private and check you over. I need some time with my mate to reassure my wild side and I know Kotah does too."

I nod. "Sounds good. You didn't, by chance, find my phone at the house did you? I know I burned up my sexy snowman, but I was hoping I didn't kill my cell too.

"It's in the side pocket of your go-bag in the back seat," Brant says, pulling away to open the back door. "Hop in and hand me the blanket. I'll return it to Grant and thank him."

"Oh, I should thank him too," I say, hesitating before climbing into the back seat.

"You can thank him at dinner tonight. I'm taking you home to meet the parents. I'm sure Margo and Ben are already planning a grand family dinner for us."

"Excellent," I say, climbing into the back seat and handing Brant the blanket.

The heated gaze I get from both of them sparks every pang of wanton I posses. "Hurry, back Bear. You're not the only one who needs reassurance."

Kotah closes the SUV door and is on top of me before I've finished dropping the seatback. As the seat clunks flat, I'm tearing at his shirt and he's shoving his jeans down his thighs. "I'm sorry, Calli. I can't wait."

He's got his mouth locked on my nipples and I arch into his kiss.

Me being naked already is a distinct advantage. "Don't wait. This is perfect."

Too soon, he abandons his suckling and slides down my body. The leather of the seat creaks as dig my heels in and push farther into the back to give him room.

He's hungry my wolf.

I spread my knees to increase his access. I'm a bit pretzeled but I'm not complaining. He dives face-first into my crotch with a roughness, Kotah doesn't usually possess.

Bruising fingers on the fleshy rounds of my ass raise my hips while his mouth and chin crush against my folds. A rush of heat zings to meet his tongue. He flicks the entrance of my pussy with aggressive prodding, his grinding mouth rubbing my aching clit.

My fingers lace into his hair and I grind his mouth, hungry and horny. "Fuck, yes," I gasp. "Eat me, Wolf. Gawd that feels so good."

I'm bucking against the pressure of his mouth when two fingers replace his tongue. The depth is pure heaven and I shudder against his touch.

"Fuck me," Brant says, climbing into the driver's seat. "Right here, right now, eh?"

I can't speak. I'm close and Kotah's lost his mind.

My skin is growing hot, but I don't care. Kotah is immune and I've torched the inside of vehicles before. My insides are hot and pulsing around his fingers.

"More, Wolf. Fuck me."

Lost in the sensations, I'm writhing in the perfection. His tongue pushes and plays as he shifts his hold. His fingers rub my clit and while he tongue-fucks my core.

"Mine." The wild growl of his wolf is too much.

I come hard against his mouth, the world blowing out of focus as my control is lost. I cry out, shouting his name and I'm flipped onto my stomach and penetrated from behind.

The keening pulse of my orgasm doesn't end but takes another crazy run at me as he slams deep into my womb. I press my forehead against the leather, bracing my palms against the folded seat as I come apart again.

All the while, his thumb is testing, probing the tight flesh of my ass. After my orgasm dies down, he withdraws and swipes the moisture from our joining to the back. "I want to fuck you here," his wolf says, penetrating me with his thumb. "When Jaxx is inside me, it's incredible. I need to mark you."

I wriggle my butt in the air and he accepts the invitation.

He prods and plays in the moisture until he gains access and is slick enough to pick up a rhythm. I swallow and try to catch my breath, absorbing the succulent burn of pleasure.

"You're so tight," he gasps behind me. "I won't last. Sweet heaven it's so good."

Hearing Kotah's loss of reserve is the sexiest thing *evah*. Hearing it in conjunction with the *slap-slap-slap* of each thrust and the tickle of his sac brushing my clit, is too much.

I won't last long either and I want to go off with him.

I shift to hold my weight with my shoulder and reach under my body to play with my clit and his balls. It doesn't take much. My clit is swollen and sensitive and even the brush of my fingers is enough to send us both crashing into release.

We collapse into a sweaty heap of tangled limbs and Kotah spoons me from behind. I close my eyes, and focus on getting reacquainted with oxygen. His heart is hammering against my back and it takes us both a long while before our breathing returns to normal.

"I'm so sorry, Calli." I hear the sorrow in his words and know the amped-up sex we shared was largely his wolf freaking out about my kidnapping.

I squeeze his arm around me and glance back over my shoulder. "There's nothing to be sorry about, Wolf. I'm yours. You're mine. We're both safe and together and spent. That's all there is."

He presses his lips to my shoulder and kisses me. Somehow, I don't think he heard me.

❧

## Brant

As much as it keys me up to watch Calli get thoroughly fucked by the kid, it's torture too. She's putting all her effort into moving forward with the others and I feel like I'm getting left behind. It's my own fault —I know that—but for a guy who prides himself on having a way with females, I realize now I have no clue about connecting with them on a meaningful level. Certainly nothing lasting.

Hannah may have been joking when she made fun of me 'taking it slow' but she's right. Before Calli, it was nothing for me to get inside a female twenty minutes after setting my sights on her. So, what's my problem with Calli?

"All set," Calli says, climbing into the front seat of the truck wearing one of the fire-resistant outfits Hawk had made for her. "Thanks for bringing my bag. As much as I love being naked with you guys, it's nice to have clothes available when meeting new people."

I hear the teasing tone in her voice and play along. "There's nothing wrong with being naked for first impressions. You'll always stand out in their minds."

"Right?" She's smiling, but when I look over, she's got the same tentative look in her eye as I feel. "Are you okay, Bear? Are we okay?"

"Yeah, of course. Always. I'm tired from the trip and relieved you're safe."

We ride along in silence for a few minutes before she straightens. "Oh, sorry. I should've asked. How did it go with tracking down the kids?"

"They got four of them," Kotah says from the back seat.

I nod. "Yeah, it turns out they've been separated and are being held in different locations."

She fingers through her hair and frowns. "Any leads on how to find the others?"

"I'm not sure where we are on that. Hannah and her team are taking it from here."

"Hannah, the one you texted me about?"

"The same. And though I'm sure you already know this, there's nothing between us. She's just a co-worker."

"I trust you, Bear. What does that mean, her team is taking it from here? Are you handing it over?"

I hit the indicator and make my turn toward the ranch. "Yeah. For now, I need to focus on other things closer to home. Hannah's good. I trust that she'll run with what I started and keep me informed."

She searches my expression and then smiles. "Okay. I can't say I'm disappointed to have your full attention, but I don't want you walking away from something that matters to you. I don't want our mating to cost you anything you value."

"Nah. I'm good. Focusing on the quint is my effort to bring me *closer* to what I value." I pull off the road and stop at the first gate. "Kotah, do you mind opening the gate?"

The kid jumps out, unhooks the rope latch, and walks the gate open. Then, when I drive through, he closes it back up and jumps in.

"It's not the high-tech security of anywhere Hawk would put us, but as I told him, I could've protected us too."

"And you swear he's all right?" Calli says. "Damn, I wish I'd been there. I feel so bad he's suffering."

"Jaxx says he's moving slow but he's moving. He also said he's even crankier than usual."

Calli smiles. "Lucky us."

When I get to the intersection of laneways, I take a left and follow it around the south Bisson pastures to the driving shed. I pull up to the loading door and stop. "Kotah, if you would. The code is 25118."

Kotah chuckles as he gets out to punch in the digits. "I get it."

Calli arches a brow. "And what am I missing?"

"The code is the alphanumeric value of the word bear."

She laughs. "And he caught on that fast? Man, his brain works on a different level than mine, that's for sure."

"Mine too."

When the electronics open things up, I drive the SUV inside and get out of the truck. After closing us in, I grab our bags and point toward the bags of manure stacked on skids in the corner. I chuckle at the confusion on their faces.

"Welcome to one of the Ursine safehouses."

Kotah looks around at the old tractor and the tools hanging on the board and batten walls. Opening the rusted-out electrical panel on the wall, I place my hand on the scanner.

"Access, Brantley Robbins, granted."

The motor beneath the skid hums to life and the whole stack of manure shifts to the side revealing the hatch of the old, underground military bunker. "My Alpha is a retired four-star general and one of only a dozen people who ever knew this bunker existed. He bought the land after it was decommissioned and restored it for our purposes."

I gesture for Kotah to take the lead and he slings his bag over his shoulder and starts down.

"The light is on your right, waist-high."

When the tunnel lights up, I drop Calli's bag down to him and help her get turned around and started on the ladder.

"This is very Mission Impossible, Bear."

"Keeping it interesting, beautiful."

I wait until Kotah clears her from the bottom of the ladder and follow suit. When I shut the hatch over my head, the motor hums and the skid slides back into place. "You're safe here. We have time to regroup and figure out our next move. Come on, I'll show you two around."

*Hawk*

"Go over it all again," I say twenty minutes after we take off.

Jaxx pries one eye open and shoots me a dirty look. "Some of us were up all night savin' your ass. A little shut-eye doesn't seem to be too much to ask for."

"Yeah, well, I'm trying to save all our asses. From the top, Jaguar.

Kotah's mother shows up out of the blue with no apparent reason other than to make his life miserable."

"As usual."

"As usual," I agree. Despite me not being an overtly affectionate guy, I'm sick of that woman trashing our wolf. He's a genuinely beautiful soul. "If he had her pinned and about to crush her windpipe, our boy is at the end of his rope."

"I'm sure he's better now that Calli's found. Brant said they didn't make it out of the parkin' lot before the kid was buried inside her smoothin' the rough edges."

"You two are gossipy old ladies."

"Some people talk shop—we talk sex. No details. It's all very PG."

I roll my eyes. "How did the Prima get there?"

"Palace Learjet, I suppose."

I look to Lukas. "Find out when the flight plan was filed and who ordered it."

Lukas snorts. "That's *waaay* beyond my paygrade, Barron. The Prima is our first lady."

"Tell whoever is asking that you're inquiring on behalf of the Prime-in-Waiting. Jaxx, text Kotah and make sure he's okay with that."

Jaxx pulls out his phone. "I will, but I can already tell you he won't mind. If it helps us find out who's gunnin' for Calli, he'll be on board."

"So, who else knew you were in Oregon?" Lukas asks. "I assume you booked the place with one of your usual aliases."

That sparks something. "I did but Jayne knows my aliases and had tracked our travel logs to Oregon. She called me and asked me about it while we were outside the estate awaiting confirmation."

Lukas frowns. "So, she confirmed your whereabouts immediately before a hostile attack force moved in on your mate at a secondary location?"

Jaxx's growl fills the air.

Fuck that sound is cool. *I wish hawks growled like that.*

Jaxx pegs me with an icy glare. "Hawk, if you can't leash that bitch, I will."

I nod. "I won't try to stop you. Still, we can't move until we know for sure who's acting against us. Jayne's a hostile, yes, but I don't see her undermining the FCO. She's worked long and hard to move the company forward."

"If she tracked your travel logs to Oregon, we can't just take the company helicopter and show up at the Ursine safehouse," Jaxx says. "We have to be smarter than that. That puts not only our mates in danger but also Brant's family."

"Agree." I sigh, tamping down the screech of my hawk as he realizes my intention. "Lukas, have the pilot change our destination to our corporate getaway property on Vancouver Island."

Jaxx frowns. "Canada? Seriously? Can't we figure out a way to get home to Calli to see that she's all right with our own eyes?"

"We will. I have a boat in Vancouver. We'll get there, stay a day or two to see if anyone takes the bait, and then tomorrow night or the next, we'll leave under the cover of darkness and follow the coastline down to Seattle. It'll be fine, Jaxx. Didn't you tell me we should spend time hanging out and getting to know one another?"

Jaxx huffs. "Yeah, but I didn't mean I wanted to give up three days without seeing Calli after she was just kidnapped. I need to reassure my cat that she's unharmed.."

I close my eyes. "I feel the same way. But, believe it or not, Jaguar, three days without sex won't kill either of us."

# CHAPTER ELEVEN

## Calli

*T*he Kolter ranch where Brant was raised in Washington State is a nine-hundred-acre, farm with four-hundred bison grazing over their sprawling farmland. They have a meat business, a leather business, and run agritourism events on the weekends in the summer for those who want a taste of country life. It's run by the grizzly Ursine Alpha, General Ben Kolter, and his honey bear mate, Margo.

"Call me Papa Bear. Everybody does."

My hand is swallowed up by Brant's foster father the moment we arrive. As impossible as it seems, I'd bet in his prime, Ben was even bigger and brawnier than Brant. "It's good to meet you, sir."

"And this is Margo. Our den mother," Brant says, gesturing to the women with gray-streaked brown hair and kind, denim blue eyes. She's dressed in a cotton t-shirt, worn, faded jeans, and dirty boots. Hard-working. No airs. I like her immediately.

"It's a pleasure."

Margo takes my hand and pulls me into a hug. "The pleasure is ours, Calli. We've only been able to get snippets of news from Brant about the quint and what's been going on. We were so worried when he just drove off that first day. A phoenix rising. It shook our understanding of what we thought we knew but I bet it did the same for you five on a much larger scale."

I chuckle. "You'd win that bet. I didn't even know about the existence of fae or wildlings or any of it. Those first days weren't my best and brightest."

"Nonsense," Brant says, hugging my shoulder. "She's been our beacon since that first moment."

I roll my eyes and laugh. "Your pants are on fire, Bear."

Next, it's Kotah's turn to face the in-laws. I don't know if they are aware of Kotah's status as Fae royalty. Since the morning after his Prime in Waiting swearing-in ceremony, he's taken the time and effort to conceal the Fae Prime tattoo branded into his cheekbone. He also wears the black, leather choker over the royalty band tattooed around his throat.

To anyone who doesn't know his station, he simply looks like a handsome wolf wildling with wonderful posture and amazingly long hair.

Brant's parents must know his station though because the exuberance they showed in shaking my hand and hugging me is gone and they make no move to touch him.

I catch the hurt as it flashes in his eyes.

Brant must've caught it too, because he pulls him close and kisses the side of his head. "And this is Kotah, our wolf. He's the brains of the operation and the soul of our family."

"It's a pleasure to meet you, son," Papa Bear says.

*Please hug him,* I think, repeating it in my head. Physical contact with the royal family is forbidden, but Kotah craves the affection so badly it breaks my heart.

Margo and Ben don't seem sure what they're allowed—

"Group hug," Brant says, ending the hesitation and folding us all into the massive arms of him and his alpha. "Bears are big huggers," he says, making sure his foster parents come in contact with him. "And we're family now. S'all good."

Margo takes the hint and gives Kotah a hug. "It's a pleasure, Wolf. Brant speaks so highly of you."

A wild ringing from the front porch of the main house brings our attention to the teenaged blonde girl striking the inside of a triangle with the metal wand. "Supper's up."

Brant smiles and pats his stomach. "Excellent. I could definitely eat."

I laugh. "Is there ever a time when you turn down food?"

"No." Margo and Ben both say at once.

The five of us are still chuckling when we enter the house. Brant takes us into the laundry room off the main entrance and we wash our hands. The room smells like a mixture of laundry detergent and bison manure. My guess is they come in here straight from the barn and shuck off their work clothes before they tromp through the house.

Good plan. It's not a smell I'd want in my bedroom.

Maybe I'm too much of a city girl to appreciate it.

Dinner is a chaotic affair of close to thirty bears making plates and settling at the table, the island, and in the adjoining family room and den. A cacophony of cutlery clinking plates, chairs scraping, laughter, and people talking over each other is like nothing I've ever experienced.

Then again. The biggest family I've ever had is now with the five of us.

"I was so relieved Grant introduced himself at that field. I didn't know if I was in Oregon or Maine and am only learning the different fae species and their alignments. To say I felt exposed would be an understatement... and that's without being naked."

Margo hugs grant from behind his chair and kisses his cheek. "Well done. The Fates were with us today."

"That they were," Brant says, holding up his wineglass. "We're forever in your debt, my friend."

~

88

After dinner, Papa Bear takes Brant and Kotah out to the barn to help him with a problem he's having with a feed chute and I'm left for some private time with Margo.

She hands me a stack of small plates and a handful of spoons and forks. "Help me get dessert sorted for the horde and then the five of us will be able to eat ours in peace and quiet when they're done in the barn, yeah?"

Peace and quiet sound wonderful.

The young blonde girl, Hadley, carries the pies and Margo's got a chocolate cake as well as a cheesecake. I set the plates and cutlery down and shake my head. "You didn't need to go to all this trouble for us. I'm so thankful just to be here."

Margo laughs. "Oh, honey. This spread is the same as we had last night and the night before that. Bears eat. You get twenty-seven of them in one place, you need the food to fill them. But be sure, we're happy to have you here too. Brant's special to us. We wanted a chance to meet his new family."

I look at all the food and can't imagine what their grocery bills must be. No wonder they're bison farmers. They must have to fill their freezer with meat they grow themselves.

"I'm sorry Jaxx and Hawk missed out," Margo says. "It's quite the cross-section you have in your quint. A lot of strong personalities to blend."

While she cuts the cheesecake, I cut the pies. "We've had a few bumps but it's coming together better now."

"Brant and your corporate raider collide I'm sure."

I nod. "Yeah, Hawk seems to rub Brant the wrong way about almost everything."

"Be patient with him. He's not one for authority figures or people making decisions that affect him. He's hard-headed and opinionated, but he has a good heart and he gets there in the end."

"Is that because of something in his childhood or has he always been like that?"

Margo shrugs. "Nothing that happened here that I know of. And honestly, we know very little of his life before he was found and brought to us. Either he can't remember much or he refused to talk about it, we never could tell. Eventually, we let it alone and focused him on looking toward the future."

I follow her lead and start making plates and pushing them toward the end of the table where the ice cream, whipped cream, and several sugary toppings are. "What was he like as a cub? I imagine him as a bit of a scamp getting into things and getting the others in trouble."

She laughs. "No. That was Dillan. The two of them have always been inseparable and when D got into trouble Brant was right there following along."

"Dillan? They were close?"

"Still are."

"Oh, he's never mentioned him."

Margo chuckles. "He's been with you since day one, honey. Dillan's our black bear military man."

"Doc? Oh. I guess I never asked his real name."

She nods. "Yeah, well, Brant was our introvert. I used to call him my little shadow. When he first arrived, he didn't change into his boy form for over a year. I don't know what trauma he suffered, but something cut him to the quick. I didn't even know what the boy looked like until I caught Dillan playing with him outside in the water barrel. Took me a minute to put it together, but the two have never been far apart since that day."

"An introvert. That's hard to picture. He's very social."

"Don't be fooled by the class clown routine. With Brant, you've got to look deeper."

The first wave of dessert takers pass through as we continue making up plates. "Calli, I understand it's none of my business, but from what I've dug up about the phoenix and her guardians, I figured you two would be mated by now. You wear the marking scent of the other three on you, but not his. May I ask why?"

Umm... *awkward.*

"Honestly, I don't know why. I feel like he's less committed as time passes. He's attentive and protective, but when we were first thrown together, he was all in. Now, I worry he's having second thoughts. I ask him about it and he swears everything is fine, but it isn't."

"I doubt it's anything as conscious-minded as him knowing what he's doing or why. Brant is great out of the gate but has trouble connecting. He's everybody's friend and the good-time guy but I'd say there are only three people in this world close enough to him to truly know him and that's me, Ben, and Dillan."

"I lost my parents and had a bad childhood too. He knows that. I'd think that would make it easier for him to open up to me."

Margo shrugs. "It took us years to break through Brant's defenses. Maybe being mated will speed up the process because it's more binding than us offering an orphaned boy a home, but I'd bet it'll still take him time to trust in a future with the five of you."

I sigh. According to the Fae Council and everyone weighing in, time isn't on our side. We need to align as mates and get ready for what's to come. "Thanks for the head's up."

It's late by the time we say goodnight to Brant's Alpha and the half-dozen other bears who live on the property of the Bisson farm. Apparently, Papa Bear, is a collector of lost souls. Everyone in the ursine community knows that if a wildling cub is abandoned, orphaned, or without a home, he'll take them in.

Brant was lucky to be one of his wards.

"You should've told me you grew up not knowing your parents," I say as we bump along the laneway in one of the little golf carts they use to travel on the property. "You had to know I'd understand what that's like."

He shrugs. "It's not the same as what you lived through. The people who took me in loved me. I was safe and nurtured. Sure, I don't remember much about my biological parents, but the memory of them is so distant, it doesn't hurt. I consider myself lucky to be part of this family."

"So, you didn't want me to feel bad because what didn't work out for me worked out great for you?"

His smile is sad, and I don't understand it. "Something like that."

"Are you sure Kotah's going to be all right?" I ask searching the darkness for any sign of my wolf.

"Will he be safe to run the acreage for the night? Absolutely. Will he bounce back from the encounter with his mother and his trauma of feeling responsible for your capture? I don't know. Likely, not any time soon."

"My poor, sweet prince," I say, staring through the fencing of the fields, wishing I could catch a glimpse of him before we lock ourselves in for the night. I press a hand on the ache in my chest. "I love him so much."

"It shows. He knows it too." Brant gets out of the cart and keys in the code so we can park our little cart before heading back down to the bunker.

"Can we leave some blankets down in case he comes back and he's locked out?"

"Sure." Brant opens a tall cupboard in the corner and takes out two thick horse blankets. "He has the code to get in here and I told him if he wants me to unlock the hatch, he can use the intercom."

I sigh. "I know. He said he wants time to himself. I'm just worried about him."

Brant does his scanner thing and opens our way and a couple of minutes later we're sealed into the bunker for the night. We walk, shoulder to shoulder and the tension is weirdly palpable.

"You tired?" he asks as we come to the end of the tunnel and enter the eight-bedroom living quarters.

"No. Full from dinner, but not tired."

"Would you like a drink? We can shoot some pool in the games room and share a bottle of red."

"Sure." In truth, I'll accept any offer he makes. I need him to let me in. "I'm pretty good at pool, though. You might be sorry you asked."

The deep bass of his laughter feels strained.

It doesn't matter. We have the next twelve hours to ourselves.

Surely by tomorrow morning, I'll know what's up with us. At least, I pray I will.

The games room is furnished with all the testosterone-infused favorites: pool, foosball, darts, ping-pong, a projector screen TV, video consoles, and a bar stocked with enough booze to stay down here for two years if we need to.

I pick my cue and grab the chalk. "Do you want to break or shall I?"

"Ladies choice."

"Okay, I'll break, you grab that wine you offered." While he trots over to the bar, I take out the triangle and rack them up. "What are the stakes?"

He chuckles again. "Do we need stakes?"

"Oh, yeah, I think we do." I rock the balls forward and position the yellow on the button. "How about... for every ball sunk the other player has to speak one truth or answer one question."

Brant comes back to the table with two flutes and a bottle. "That sounds harmless enough. Get us started."

Leaning over the end of the table, I line up my shot and crack the cue ball into the house. Both back corners shoot straight into the pockets.

Brant's eyebrow shoots up. "You rigged the rack."

"Says you. If you were worried about cheating, you should've checked the setup."

He chuckles. "Okay, am I offering two answers or are you asking two questions?"

I already know what I want to ask. "I know it's been asked and answered, but under the oath of pool etiquette, you have to speak truthfully. Are we okay, Bear? You say we are but that's not at all how it feels. If you're having second thoughts about me and the mating, I need you to be straight with me. Just be honest."

Brant's expression tightens. "Wow. You're not messing around." He tips back his glass of wine and draws a deep breath. "I don't know what's wrong with me, honestly. I think you're incredible. I want to connect. I want this mating to work but I keep making excuses to focus everywhere else."

He gestures between the two of us. "I said I wanted it to be private and special our first time. That was true but since when have I ever cared about that? Then I got so caught up with my distrust for Hawk, I acted like a jackass."

"True story."

"My logic was sound, but my judgment was off. I'm usually smarter than that."

"Everyone has their moments."

"And the entire time since you resurrected, I've been obsessed with finding those kids and I realized last night when you were taken that none of that is real."

He leans his ass against the air hockey table and drinks more wine. "I considered myself a lady's man. Yeah, I treated them right and thought I had it going on, but when I think about the ones who came before you, not one of them moved beyond 'a good time for a short time'. I've never had one meaningful relationship. I'm not sure I even know how."

"You do," I say sipping from my glass and then setting it on the floor instead of on the felt of the table. Standing directly in front of him, I reach up and clasps my fingers at the back of my neck. "I see you, Bear. I see your strength… and I'm not talking about your big, manly muscles. Your truest strength is how deeply you care for strangers. Like me when we first mated and I was lost, like the plethora of women who came before me, and like those kids you know are out there and in danger."

"But that's where things shut down."

I smile, understanding him for the first time. "You have deep relationships with the other bears in your sleuth."

"That's easy. They're my family."

"No. They weren't. Your family was taken from you at a young age. These bears were the people who stepped in and filled that emptiness. They *became* your family because you let them in. You trusted that they weren't going to leave you and I'm guessing that took a great deal of time."

He shrugs. "I guess. I never really thought about it."

I step back, take his hand, and grab the bottle of wine. "Come with me. I'm suggesting our next pastime and it involves a lot less clothing."

# CHAPTER TWELVE

Jaxx

"Swanky digs, avian," I say, taking a wandering stroll through the main floor of the FCO team-building retreat. It's a thirty-six-thousand square foot bungalow with a workout center, a private theater, and an indoor pool. "At least if we're suffering, we're suffering in style."

Hawk chuckles and eases himself down on one of the couches. "Glad you approve. If you don't mind, I think I might lose consciousness now."

"You do you, mate. I'm house-trained. I know how to make myself at home and behave." I leave Hawk to his goals of comatose and venture off to find the pool. I've just discovered the glassed-in room when Lukas tracks me down.

"Headed for a swim?" he asks.

"Yeah, after a few laps do you wanna scrounge up some grub? I'm getting hungry. Any good restaurants in the neighborhood that might deliver?"

"I've called in the private chef for this location. Do you have any food allergies, preferences, or must-haves?"

*Private chef... schmancy.* "Nope. I'm an easy houseguest. I like Mexican, American, Italian, Indian, Greek..."

"In other words, food."

I grin. "Yep. That covers it. Food is good."

"And, where is he?"

I throw my thumb over my shoulder the way I came. "Taking a time-out on the living room sofa."

"Good. He needs it. I have a couple of things to follow up on in the office suite. If you run into a black man that looks like a former pro boxer, that's the chef. His name is Milo. Leave him to do his thing. He doesn't like people in his kitchen while he's cooking."

"Fair enough. I don't want to piss off the man preparing my meals especially if he can kick my pussy ass."

Lukas chuckles. "I put your duffle in the first bedroom past the theater. When you've dried off and are dressed, find me and we'll recap what we know over some chow. I promise to protect you from Milo."

"Sounds good. And thanks, Lukas. Hawk strives to take good care of us, but I know you're his right-hand man working behind the scenes. We owe you."

Lukas dips his chin. "My pleasure. You four are good for him. When all is said and done, the universe knew what it was doing putting you five together. He may not say it in so many words, but he thinks so too."

I place my hand on my chest, comforted by the warmth of my soul shard beneath my palm. "I couldn't agree more. Now it's just a matter of putting theory into practice and getting him to engage... in a non-hostile way."

Lukas chuckles. "Good luck."

*Kotah*

I run beneath the light of the moon, my claws tearing into the pastureland of Brant's family home. The herd is grazing in the eastern fields and I promised Papa Bear I wouldn't spook them. I stay on the west side of the farm, thankful for the open space and the smell of clean air.

In truth, it's clean air tainted with the pungency of bison manure, but at least it's a natural scent.

I launch over a gully and my heart stutters as a jackrabbit takes flight to my right. My belly is full, but the pull of the chase is too much to ignore. I seize the distraction, course-correct, and let my wolf loose to enjoy the chase.

Unlike in my forested Northwood home, the trees here are sparse and too spread out to offer Bugs any real escape. We dodge the intermittent trunks, jumping the exposed roots, and barrel through the long, wild grass.

I need this. Out here, the wind blows through my coat and I am one with my environment. There is no royal obligation or betrayal of parents or failure to save my beloved.

Out here there is only the law of nature.

That I understand.

When all else fails, that makes sense to me.

Another bouncing lunge and I snap my jaws close to Bugs's tail. He kicks back at me and gives an extra boost. After another few minutes, I take pity on my racing partner and lunge wide, giving him the chance to dart away and hide.

I don't slow. I abandon the hunt and push my muscles. I need to be better prepared, better equipped, and better suited to stand as a Guardian of the Phoenix.

I lift my muzzle, breath sawing in and out of my heaving lungs. My muscles burn but my mind is finally emptying. As much as I love my mates, when things hit too close to home, I need solitude to quiet my mind.

I need to run.

*Brant*

"Is the view doing anything for you, Bear?"

I bark a laugh and lean further into the molded seat at my back. Without apology, I take in Calli's open-leg display as she sits on the top edge of the hot tub. "You blow my mind, beautiful. There's nothing wrong with the appeal. I want you. You want me. It should be as simple as that."

"Then we take it as slow as you want until you believe in it. I don't mind slow, as long as I know what page we're on."

"*I* don't even know what page I'm on. But it has nothing to do with not being ball-throbbing hot for you."

She smiles and slides into the water, the globes of her boobs glistening as they bob to the top of the surface. She takes the seat opposite me and reaches her arms flat on the back of the tub behind her. "Well, we had dinner, I met your folks, and now we have all night to be naked together and get comfortable with one another."

Her legs straighten under the water and she fondles my junk with her toes. "You get to say how much and when to stop. I'm hoping we can flirt a little… and maybe make out a lot. If that's all you're up for, I'm happy to take the journey with you."

I capture her feet and close my legs, bringing her heels into my lap to massage her feet. "I don't want you pussy footing around me. There's no conscious desire to put on the brakes. I'm as hungry for you as the others."

"I get that. My point stands. I'm not going to ambush you like I did to Hawk. He needed to get over himself and get out of his own way. I'm giving you the reins."

I bend down and lift her toes above the bubbling water to give them a nip. "Is that a carte blanche invitation?"

She waggles her brows. "Hells yeah."

I lean back and settle in. This is going to be a good night. "Okay, then let's get comfortable with one another."

"Where do you want to start?"

"Sexual fantasies."

She shrugs. "I've been living those the past few weeks. Multiple guys. Male/male voyeurism. Being ravished anywhere and anytime the urge hits. What about you?"

"I've been too long on the sidelines. I want to start being part of the game."

"Anything you want to share?"

I chuckle and lick my lips. "How crude is too crude?"

She giggles and her boobs bob. "Oh, I don't get offended by crude. I'm not a fan of the 'C' word, but other than that, nothing makes me cringe."

"Alright. Honestly, I want you to ride my face and cream in my mouth. I want to fuck you on every surface I see, powering inside you until you can't take anymore. I want Kotah in your ass and both of you on your backs while I crawl inside you. I want you to suck my cock until I cum hard in your mouth and fill your belly. I want to be on my knees while Jaxx fucks me while I'm fucking you. I want all of us naked and playing with no expectations. I've even pictured myself sucking off Hawk well enough that the guy misses a beat. He might be an asshole, but that motherfucker is hot. Those tats and piercings —fuck me."

Calli's teeth capture her bottom lip. "That is a big list."

I chuckle and stroke my cock under the water. I'm harder than I've ever been, knowing where this is going. I may not be a hundy percent confident on one level, but I know where we're ending up tonight. "Talking like this is making me really, fucking horny."

Heat flares in her gaze and a ring of fire ignites around the pupils of her eyes. Her phoenix burns stronger every day. The fact that she got air yesterday is incredible.

She swallows and I watch her stiff nipples peek out of the water as the jets cycle off. The bubbles clear and the water falls still. Her gaze drops and she now sees the proof of exactly how horny I am. "So, when do you anticipate starting your sexy to-do wish list…"

I growl and push forward, meeting her as she launches and collides with me in the middle. "Right now."

*Calli*

Brant's list does in my self-control. I initiated the hot tub experience to increase intimacy without expectation. That flies out the window when he makes me imagine all the things he wants to do to me—with me. I'm crushed against his solid chest as he lifts me into his arms and carries me out of the steamy water.

The air is cold on my heated flesh and I shiver in his arms. "Give me two minutes, beautiful. I'll warm you up with friction."

I snuggle into his massive frame and kiss his pec. The sharp muscled ridges of his powerful animal side cushion the softness of my own. Not that I'm as soft as I used to be. Daily workouts and the progression of my wildling side have sculpted my body over the past three weeks.

"So, that whole speech I gave you on taking it slow... I want you to know I do mean it."

The grin that breaks his lips has my core pulsing for attention. "We're not waiting. I'm beyond desperate right now."

"Thank gawd."

The vibration of his laughter against my chest is a sexy friction. Grabbing two fluffy towels off the pile, he flips them into my lap and heads out of the hot tub area. "The biggest problem I face now is where to begin my feast. I hunger for so much."

"Then consider me your smorgasbord."

"I appreciate your commitment to the cause," he says, taking a left and stopping in the doorway to the kitchen. He studies the layout of the room, and then his grin widens.

My pussy pulses with anticipation.

He sets my feet on the floor and I lean against the kitchen island. I yip at the cold marble against my ass and he chuckles.

"Thus, the towels." After unfurling them onto the floor, he lays on his back and smacks his lips. "Sit on my face and hold onto the counter to keep steady."

Laid out like this, his physical perfection is too beautiful to believe. All this is mine? A rush of cream heats my core and I groan. "Make me, Bear."

His brow arches. "You wanna play that game?"

"Who's playing. You hold the reins remember. If you want it, you have to take it."

The growl that rumbles from deep in his chest nearly makes me come. He sits up and with a control of strength I'm sure only he could manage, he lifts me off my feet, splits my knees and lays back down with me straddled over his mouth. *"Bon appetite."*

My eyes roll back in my head as he grips my hips and angles my core to his best advantage. There are no sweet sweeps of lips and tongue and butterfly kisses. Brant devours my clit and grinds his mouth against me with a heated madness that vibrates across our bond.

"Fuck yeah. Feed me, Calli. I'm thirsty."

I grip the cantilevered surface of the breakfast bar and steady myself. The towels are soft under my knees, but the stubble of his day's growth brushes against my folds in a rough ecstasy. I close my eyes and focus on the sensation of his mouth. There's no hesitation now. Maybe powering through his subconscious hesitation is the way to go.

I'm up for trying. Yeah, this, for as long as it takes.

Pleasure tingles over my skin and I drop my head back and focus on my breathing. I won't pass out tonight. No matter how wild things get... no passing out.

One of his hands releases my hips and I hear the wet *snick-snick-snick* of precum tossing behind me.

"Are you stroking off."

He shifts position to speak and I instantly regret asking him a question. "I gotta take the edge off or I'm going to split you wide when I get inside you."

He gets back to it, and my world is happy once more.

He's very good at multi-tasking and I don't want to think about how he got so adept at eating pussy.

His tongue penetrates, his lips are sloppy and wet as he feeds his frenzy. His bear is growling now, the violent slap of his masturbating nearing completion.

It's so hot. I've seen him satisfy himself more than once. I can picture the tension in his abs and pecs, the way his whole body shudders with the violence of him coming hard.

A hot keening lights up deep inside me and I call the feeling forward. I want to lose my mind. I want to come into his mouth like he wants. He groans and his arm tightens around my thigh, pinning me to his mouth and pressing the pads of two fingers on my clit.

He barely makes contact and I'm convulsing, rocking against his tongue, gasping as my head falls back. My phoenix writhes inside me, eager to claim her last mate.

"It's so good," I gasp, riding out the pulsing waves.

Wildly engaged, my throaty cry is still in the air when the world spins. Brant's on his feet and we're chest to chest. His arms are around me and my legs wrap around his hips. The swollen tip of his cock presses hot against my entrance and I understand his concern from a moment earlier.

Brant's cock is big—like really big—without a doubt, the biggest I've ever had.

Pressing my back against the wall, he starts a slow swivel of his hips, pressing and probing. I feel the silky sheath sliding over solid steel as I try to catch my breath.

My pulse thunders hard in my veins. His care and concern in a moment when we're both so incredibly turned on is touching but also maddening. I wriggle my hips, to hurry the process, and hide the wince the stretching causes.

"No, baby. Let me take it slow. I don't want to hurt you."

"I'm a phoenix, Bear. If I tear a little, I'll heal right back up… and honestly, I don't mind a little pleasure-pain."

Either he's not hearing me or he's not listening.

"Seriously, Brant. Stop playing the part of the gentleman. I need you inside me. Fuck your mate."

# CHAPTER THIRTEEN

Brant

*J*'m trying to maintain control here, but I'm losing my mind. The need to mark Calli inside and out is stronger now than it's been for the past weeks—and that's saying something. Even after taking the edge off, my wood is still more like a fucking sequoia. It's carnal. It's barbaric. It's undeniable.

Calli squirms in my hold. She's a greedy and impatient little fireball. My cock probes the damp heat of her pussy, and I can't breathe. Can't think.

"Bear, please."

Right. She'll heal. I push inside her, and though I mean to only enter her a bit and wait for her to adjust, I can't stop. I thrust fully and bury myself in the grip of her core.

"Oh, fuck," she screams in a throaty cry.

"I'm sorry," I say, hating myself for rushing this. "I didn't want to hurt you."

"You're not," she gasps, the lush curves of her breasts heaving, her fingers digging into my shoulders. She leans back and I watch those beautiful rounds rise and fall. She groans as I withdraw and fill her again. "You fill me, yes"—her eyes roll back—"but it's wonderfully invasive. I bet mates are well-suited in more ways than habit and temperament because this is perfection."

Maybe she's right. The fit is incredible.

Gripping the back of my neck, she pulls my lips to hers and invades me too. Her tongue dances in my mouth and battles against mine. I growl, and the sound is more beast than man.

Calli isn't dainty or shy, I knew that. And now that we got my stalling jitters out in the open, there's no reason to hold back. Calli likes bold and commanding. Wild.

I can be wild for her. I *am* wild for her.

I pump my hips and my body finally overtakes my mind. Her inner muscles grip me tight, greedy for more. I press my mouth against her neck and hammer inside her.

"Yes, Bear. This. Give me all of you."

Fuck. If this is mating sex, I never want it to end.

I nip the skin of her throat and energy explodes between us. Something in our bond builds. It courses between us, swirling from my system to hers and back again.

The connection we share intensifies like it used to be made of string but now is a steel cable. It's like plugging into her has somehow merged us as one.

Well, physically, yeah, it has, but it's more than that.

Calli's skin heats and the charred scent of her phoenix fills my senses. Fire licks over my skin but it doesn't burn or cause me pain. I thrust deeper, faster, my need to be inside her multiplying into crazy territory.

It's sweet succulence—the best kind of torture.

My growl is loud and long and vibrates between us.

"Oh, gawd, yes!" Calli arcs against my hold and bucks like she's shattering in my arms. "Growl. Fuck me and growl."

The world explodes into nothing but instinct. My bear ascends and growls for her. She screams and comes unglued, her nails digging into the flesh of my shoulders.

Sweat drips into my eyes and I close them tight, pumping into her with insane power. How am I not splitting her in two? It has to be the mating magic because Calli's screaming in ecstasy and her inner muscles are greedily milking my cock.

My muscled legs stiffen as my balls tighten and burn. I press forward, crushing our bodies together, and come harder than I thought possible. My breath catches and I spill into her.

My bear roars with each hot pulse of cum, the animal in me relishing the marking. "*Mine.*"

I've watched Kotah and Jaxx as they lose their load. I could see it was incredible but never imagined this. Breath heaving, thighs trembling, the smell of sweat and sex mingling in the air, I carry us, still joined, to the sofa in the living room.

"Are you going to carry me naked and sex me in all the rooms?" she asks, her eyes crinkling at the sides with her smile.

I sink onto the sofa with her straddled over my hips and riding my lap. It takes a minute for my breathing to steady and my heart to stop threatening to burst. When I can speak again, I run my thumb over the tight tip of her nipple.

"The idea has merit. We've got about ten hours before I have to share you. Let's give it a shot."

She grins, flashing me a look with half-masted emerald eyes. "I love how you boys don't need to pace yourselves."

I push up with my pelvis and she groans. "I love how you heal, so you won't get sore."

I stick my thumb in her mouth and let her suck on it for a bit, then I reach down between our joined bodies and find the tight nub of her clit. "Wildling males are machines once we're mated. When you've had enough of me, you'll have to let me know. Otherwise, I may never let you off my cock. I'm certainly never letting you get dressed."

"That might be awkward with your alpha at breakfast."

I suck in a breath as she grips my shoulders and swivels her hips, initiating a slow rock. I'm not the only one ready to go again. The sweet scent of her arousal calls to every instinct I've got. Yep. I might give up the rest of my life and devote myself solely to pleasuring my mate.

Jaxx, Kotah, and Hawk better be ready to share because I've got to get me more of this.

*Jaxx*

It's late when I'm woken by another raging hard-on and give up on sleep. I miss my mates… especially with them banging like rabbits all night long. Don't get me wrong, I'm stoked that Brant and Calli are finally connecting, it's just killing me to feel the sexual mojo while I'm so far away from them.

I pull on my boxers and head to the kitchen for a beer. Hawk isn't on the couch, so I make him a sandwich and grab him a beer too. The guy had been so out of it all afternoon, Lukas and I let him sleep through dinner.

Wildling physiology is stronger than human, but no matter how you cut it, the guy suffered multiple gunshots and narrowly missed punching his ticket.

When I get to Hawk's room, I tap lightly on the door. "Hey, boss man, you decent?" When nothing comes back to me, I shift my load and open the door a crack.

The bed's been used but he's not there.

I'm about to duck out and track him down when my instincts kick in and my mating bond lights up. Our connection has been twanging all night, bombarded with the sexcapades of Calli and Brant, so I've been shutting it out.

I open up and access my connection to Hawk.

Okay, he's not dead. That's good.

The whispered cursing coming from the bathroom isn't a great sign though. After setting down the sandwich and beers, I close the door to the hall. Alphas react badly showing weakness in front of others.

Whether he's comfortable with it, or not, I'm his mate. I'm not sure how he'll feel if Lukas pops his head in here.

"Knock, knock," I say, pushing the bathroom door open. "Anybody need a paramedic?"

Hawk looks up at me from the tub and I know in an instant things aren't going his way. His color is off, he's shivering, and his lips are blue. "I wanted the feel of blood and death off of my skin."

The tub is one of those elegant free-standing numbers which is good. It means I have great access to get him out of there. I take a knee beside the basin and press my fingers to the inside of his wrist. "Christ, Hawk, you're a popsicle."

He's shivering bad and I drop a hand into the water. "Okay, first things first, why are you taking an ice bath?"

He rolls his eyes and I'm glad he still has the strength to be annoyed. "It was warm when I got in... Getting in was easier than getting out."

Yeah... he's too fucking weak to pull himself out.

Reaching to the faucets at his feet, I pull the drain plug and run the hot water. "Okay, first, we'll warm you up and wash you off. Then, I'll get you back into bed."

The hostile look he shoots me makes me smile.

"Hawk. I'm a paramedic. Being a caregiver when people are at their worst is what I do. You're my mate. Let me take care of you."

Any other time, I know he'd fight me. The fact that he doesn't says a lot about how shitty he feels. I swirl the hot water in with the cold and start scooping it up his body.

"Fuck, that feels so good."

When the water level rises to cover him again, I shut things off. There is a washcloth and soap on the side of the tub, so I lather up and get to it. "You know, I don't sponge bath just anyone. You should feel special."

His eyes roll shut and I'm pretty sure it's more about exhaustion than being rapt with pleasure. "Skip the sponge bath. Let me warm up and then get me out of this death bowl."

I chuckle and continue my ministrations. "How sensitive is your skin? Is the pressure all right?"

"It's fine. It's also unnecessary."

"Humor me. I've been where you are. The scent of my own blood on my body made my jaguar nuts. I get it. Let me do this for you."

Over the next few minutes, he relaxes a little. I wipe down his neck and collarbones, his shoulders, and arms. When I get to his chest, I inventory his artwork and piercings. "The tats are spank, my man."

I keep things clinical, though, if truth be told, I totally want to make this rubdown more thorough and take things south. His erection is a beautiful thing. "Well, you're not so dead that Calli and Brant aren't affecting you too."

He chuffs, but his eyes remain closed. "I was having one helluva recovery nap until they started going at it."

I chuckle and finish by rinsing him down. "I know. I was lost in dreamland and woke up humping the mattress. I took care of it twice already but have been through this before. Palm priming isn't a permanent fix."

"You went through this with Kotah and me too?"

I pull the plug and wring out the cloth. Getting to my feet, I snatch a couple of towels off the vanity and wait as the water drains. I pat him dry up top and when the water is gone, I give him the towel to work on his lower half.

"Shared mate sex-drive is the gift that keeps giving. I don't pick up any moments of solo satisfaction, so I think we're safe there, but as soon as two or more of us are involved, the bond starts ringing my bell. And when I say bell, I mean my rock hard cock."

Moving to stand behind him, I ease him forward, bend my knees, and hook my arms under his. "You're up on one, 'kay? Three… two… one."

I get Hawk to his feet, wrap the second towel around his hips to stave off the chill he's still fighting, and get him out of the tub. "Do you want me to carry you?"

"Fuck you."

I chuckle and wrap my arm around his back. The bed is about a mile away, and we begin the old man shuffle. "You could totally fuck me if you wanted to. You're the cock-blocker in this relationship." He tenses and I shake my head. "Take a joke, Hawk. I'm not into necrophilia. I like my sexual partners to be able to stand on their own at the very least."

"You're an asshole."

"No. You're too worked up about your asshole."

The two of us shuffle inch by inch, covering the distance without saying anything more. I get him into bed, prop up his pillow, and serve him his snack. "You gotta keep your strength up. You missed one helluva dinner. That Milo guy is a Rockstar."

Hawk doesn't respond. He does, however, finish his sandwich and his beer without complaint. When he shifts down and pulls the blankets up to his neck, I push my luck.

I shut off the lights and climb onto the bed behind him. "Before you protest and lose your shit, I'm here to offer body heat. You're practically hypothermic after your stint in that tub. I won't slip you a pickle to go with your sandwich."

To my utter surprise, Hawk barks a laugh. "Seriously? Did you say that?"

I spoon in behind him and make sure there is plenty of space and bunched up blanket between my crotch and his ass. Then I pull the duvet over us and cocoon us in.

"Like it or not, we're both sporting steel rods because of Calli and Brant. I can't help that any more than you, but I promised you before, I respect your limits. You're safe with me. Now close your eyes and think warm thoughts. Sun-drenched beaches. Barbecuing in the summer heat. Hot showers with our phoenix."

He groans. "That one doesn't help with the cock rocket problem."

I chuckle. "Okay, erase that last one. Stick with barbecuing on the beach. Get some sleep, mate. You'll feel better tomorrow, I promise."

"Goodnight, Jaxx... and thanks."

I close my eyes and smile, wrapping my arms around him a little tighter.

# CHAPTER FOURTEEN

## Calli

*I*'m lost in post-coital unconsciousness when movement in the room wakes me from my blissful sleep. Lying face-first in the pillows, I don't move when the bed dips first on one side of me and then the other. Tender hands caress my naked backside and trace the line of my spine.

"Mmm… I missed you, Wolf."

His touch reaches my shoulders and changes direction to run back down my spine. My skin tingles to awareness as he continues past my tailbone, between my legs, and into the moist heat of hours of sex. "Are you too tired?"

I wiggle my but and lift my hips to meet his fingers. "Never."

He doesn't nudge me to roll over, so I take that as an invitation to lay there and soak it all in. He nips the small of my back and kisses and licks his way back up. By the time he sweeps my hair to the side and nips the nape of my neck, my hips are grinding the mattress.

"Spread your legs for me, *Chigua*."

I do and am rewarded for my compliance. The tip of his cock

pulses against my entrance for only a second before he shifts forward and fills me.

"I'm glad Brant came up to get me. You two have been hard at it for hours. I need you like crazy."

I push up on my hands and knees to give him more room to move. "I forgot about the bond linking our need. Sorry."

"I forgive you." He bends over me, pushing inside while grabbing my breasts. My wolf is a little obsessed with the girls. He's also quite fond of doggie style. Must be the canine in him.

Brant slides in beside me and pulls me across his chest. He brushes my hair back and cups my face with his massive hands. His mouth locks on mine and I'm in heaven. My bear can kiss like nobody's business.

He shifts me again and I'm laying on top of him, my legs spread wide to straddle his hips, and Kotah building momentum behind me. His cock is hard and thick and now I'm riding his ridge and stimulating my clit.

"That's it, beautiful. Grind on me."

$\sim$

*Hawk*

I groan, waking up with my hand tugging on my straining cock and my mating bond vibrating with lust. Christ, they're at it again. I think about the one time I've been with Calli and it pisses me off. The bear is claiming a fucking marathon. I had one session and then had to get dressed and run a conference. Life is so not fair. I want a fucking marathon.

I roll onto my back and prop one arm behind my head, and send the other one beneath the blankets. Assuming the position, I'm taking things into my own hands when I remember Jaxx. *Fuck.*

My eye pop wide and yep, there he is, naked and pulling the same rub and tug action in the chair beside the bed. If I weren't a wildling, I wouldn't be able to see him, but I am... and I do.

"I didn't want to wake you," he says, a crooked smile lifting one side of his mouth. "They're at it again."

"Yeah," I say, temporarily at a loss. My hand stalled out the moment I discovered I wasn't alone, but watching Jaxx... yeah, I resume the pleasuring. "Is this weird?"

He groans and slides a little further down the seat of the chair, manspreading like you read about. "Just two sex-deprived mates tossin' off together. What's weird about that?"

I chuckle, but the way he says it and the way his turquoise gaze seems to almost glow in the darkness does something strange to me.

"I'm not gay." The words blurt out and I'm not even sure why I say them.

He doesn't seem offended. It's all about a smooth, confident stroke with him. "Me either. Ask Calli... or better yet, join us sometime and see for yourself."

Unbidden images of that flash in my head. I grip tighter and my abs start to clench and roll.

"But you enjoy men."

"I enjoy sharing my body with the people I care about. Whether they have boy or girl parts is irrelevant. Broaden your perspective, Hawk. You're pride yourself on being a visionary. You don't need to put a label on us."

Broaden my perspective? I think of all the sexual encounters I've been part of in my life and can't believe someone is saying that to me. Yet still... "Why do you think I stumble when it comes to sex with you and the others?"

"Do you find us attractive?"

I laugh. "You ask as we're sharing a session of mutual masturbation." I take in all the subtle nuances in front of me. His sultry gaze, how the tip of his cock pulses free of his grip with every downstroke, the spicy scent of his arousal—he lets off a throaty purr, and I almost cum.

He reads my response and smiles.

*Asshole.* "Yes, fine. If I'm being honest, I think you're sexy as fuck."

Jaxx stands up and saunters over to the bed. I stiffen, ready to protest when he grabs a pillow, throws it against the footboard, and settles in facing me. "Then, in the spirit of honesty, I'll admit that I moved to the chair to keep from grindin' you. I woke up because of Calli and the others, but it's you who I'm imaginin' right now."

"I don't know what to do with that."

"But I know what to do with that." He points to my seeping cock and I close my eyes before I lose it.

"What are you doing?"

"Nothin' you don't ask for. You're a Dom. Tell me what you want, Hawk. There's just you and me here. We're consenting adults behind closed doors. Tell me what appeals to you. Do you want to sit here and watch like we are? Do you want to share the handjobs? Do you want me to suck you off? Have you ever had a cock in your mouth?"

I swallow. "No."

"You're missing out. How can you say you don't like something if you've never tried it?"

I chuckle. "We're not talking about broccoli."

"Do you like it rough? Giving it hard."

"Ah... yeah, I do."

"Male on male can be wild and rough. You don't have to worry about hurting me. You can be as rough as you want."

*Fuck me.* Why is this turning me on so much?

I don't want that, do I?

"Get out of your head, Hawk," he says, casting his alpha voice at me. "It's just you and me behind the locked door. Tell me what you want."

"I, uh... fuck, I don't know." All that tanned skin, and the chiseled blond thing going on, and then there's the swagger in his hips when he moves.

Jaxx is a predator on the prowl.

Why do I feel like his prey?

"I want... shit, I think I want you to broaden my perspective. I want you to suck my cock."

The smile on his face makes me want to take it back... but I can't...

because I do. "Yeah. I want you to suck my cock and I might want to suck on yours too."

"Be sure, Hawk. You don't get to regret this tomorrow."

"I'm sure."

"Finally," Jaxx says, shifting down the bed. Thankfully, it's a king because it takes a bit of wriggling to get things lined up. We're both on our sides and right in front of my face is—Oh *fuck!*

I thrust my hips forward as the wet heat of Jaxx's mouth sucks me in. I've always appreciated a good blowjob—who doesn't—but from the first plunge into his mouth I know this is going to stand out in my memories as one of the greatest blowjobs of all time.

It takes me a moment to settle. After all the stroking and talking, I don't want to chump out and throw off an early pearly as soon as we get started. He brings one hand between us and grips me tight, using his hold to control my depth.

I groan. "Oh, that's good."

His head bobs. His tongue flicks the opening of my weeping crown. His teeth score me with enough roughness to light me up. I breathe deep and his arousal sears me. He's genuinely getting off on getting me off.

That reality pulls me over the precipice. I grip Jaxx's erection and he pumps my hand. I give him a few strokes and then bite the bullet... or suck the cock.

It takes a second to get my bearings on pressure and depth and what he seems to like. He tastes salty and warm. And when I squeeze and stroke, drops of cum leak out.

I lap them up, savoring the flavor.

Jaxx pops off and swallows, hammering me fast and hard with his fist. His strokes are powered with a strength that only a guy could manage. I roll onto my back, and my cells ignite. "Yeah. Please. More of that."

"As much as you want," he purrs. Rising up on his knees, he's palming me like a jackhammer and bends to take my nipple ring into his mouth. "This is so fucking hot."

He twists the ring in his teeth, sending a pinch of pain zinging straight to my balls. "Yeah, rough," I gasp, gripping the back of his hair and pulling back so it tugs the flesh of my nipple even more. "I like pain, Jaxx."

How is his arm not getting tired?

The tingling in my sac is unwelcome. "I don't want to come," I gasp. "I want more."

Jaxx's jaguar lets off a purr and I'm defenseless. I shout and kick my head back, spilling onto my clenching abs. Jaxx doesn't ease up. In fact, he switches palms, swipes his hand through the creamy mess on my belly, and pegs me with a look so hot, I convulse into another round of cum spurting.

"You still want more?" he asks. "I'll take this as far as you let me. You gotta give me those boundaries if you want them respected."

I look at the cream glistening in his fingers and want to cry. "I'm so fucking tired of boundaries and making decisions. I just want you to make me feel good."

"What are you sayin'... exactly.

"I surrender."

I can't believe those words come out of my mouth, but I won't take them back. It's a truth I've refused to see for a long while now. In so many aspects of my life, I'm the dominant one. Here, with my mate, I don't want to be in charge.

Jaxx's eyes glow as his animal prowls into power. "Lift your knees," he commands, his voice heavy with the demand of an alpha.

I do as I'm told and he deposits my cum right where I expect. I look down my body and between my legs. Jaxx is fully aroused and hungry. "Last chance, Hawk. I'm losing control here. Once I'm inside you, I'm fucking you hard and long. You're going to beg me for mercy."

My eyes roll back in my head and I swear I almost blackout. No wonder Calli passed out when he was fucking her. The guy has more power than any male should have.

"Fuck me, Jaxx. Make me beg."

Jaxx swipes my cum against my ass and plays a little. "You've had anal before, yeah? Fingers? Toys?"

"No. You're in virgin territory here, Jaguar. Congrats."

"Okay, well, you said you don't mind pain. I'm big for a first run at things. This will burn at first."

"Do it."

Lining up, he uses the tip of his cock as a tool, probing, pushing, playing. When he slides his thumb inside and starts stretching me, I'm surprised at how eager I am.

"Fuck, I can't believe I want this so badly."

"Grab your cock and give it a tug." While I'm doing that, he pushes through my resistance and then withdraws. "Again."

I give myself a stroke and he pushes deeper. Everything burns for a bit, but I love it. With one last sweep of my belly, he slicks us up and starts pumping. I buck beneath him as my body shudders. With my knees in the air, he leans harder into the back of my thighs and starts ramming me in earnest.

The forward thrust has his balls slapping my ass and both of us groan. "How rough?"

It takes a second for me to form words. "No boundaries."

*Jaxx*

The sun is bursting bright on the horizon when we finally fall sated into dehydrated heaps. I lay on my back beside him, panting, sweating, and more thoroughly worn out by a lover than I have been in ages. With Calli it's different. I never use my strength against her, with Hawk, rough and raunchy rules. Never in a million years did I think Hawk needed to be dominated as badly as he did. But yeah, he runs the world, giving up the reins for a moment must've been hella-freeing.

"Jaxx? Don't take this the wrong way... please don't, but I'd like this kept between us."

"The mating is impossible to hide. Our scents altered."

"No, not the mating..."

"Your submission?"

"Yeah. I, uh… I have a lot of people watching me, judging me based on my badass outward appearance."

"I get it. Behind closed doors, mate. I don't kiss and tell."

"Thanks."

I roll onto my hip and brush my fingers over his nipple ring. "We do this again when you're a hundy percent healed and fighting fit, yeah?"

"Damn straight." His deep-throated chuckle hits me right in the junk. "It's fun being the Dom, isn't it?"

"Damn straight." I break the contact with him before my poor cock gets another big idea. "I think I figured it out. You know, what you asked me earlier about why I think you stumbled over intimacy with the guardians."

"Yeah? What did you come up with."

"I think it's an alpha thing. You pride yourself in being the expert in all things and the idea of getting down and dirty with a beta or an omega freaked you out. They've had male on male experience, and you didn't know what to expect. Your hawk didn't want to be vulnerable like that to someone lower on the dominance hierarchy."

His eyes flutter shut. "And you were different?"

I shrug. "I don't strut my alpha like you do, but your hawk picks up on it. I think that's also why you chose to bottom. You're letting another power take over for a while. I don't think you will be able to do that with Brant or Kotah, but I think, in time, you'll be able to mate them."

I yawn and close mine as well. "That's my two cents. Now, we rest. Doctor's orders."

# CHAPTER FIFTEEN

## Calli

"C'mon, Bear. Shake your fine ass." I tap my foot against the concrete floor at the end of the bunker entrance tunnel. "I need sunlight. Stomachs to fill. Air to breathe."

Kotah joins me fresh from the shower and he shrugs. "He's not ready yet? He had first shower."

"I know, right? He's been holed up in the office all morning. I need him to let us out to start our day."

"All right. Keep your panties on," Brant says, jogging up the tunnel. "Or better yet, take them off and we can stay down here for the day."

I chuckle. "As much fun as that sounds, Kotah and I want to work on my phoenix transformation. I've mated with all four of you now, so we think my wildling side will be strong."

Kotah nods. "If we can prevent you from crashing to the earth and breaking every bone in your body, I say we practice as much as possible."

"This," I say, pointing at my wolf. "I'm hoping to eliminate crash and burn from my skillset. I'm jazzed. I really think my phoenix is stronger."

"I'd like to take all the credit, but it might also have to do with what Jaxx and Hawk were getting up to." Brant raises his brow and shakes his head. "Still can't picture that."

That's another reason I want outside. I need to phone them. I want the details. "Oh, I've been picturing it for hours," I say. "What I want now is to witness it firsthand."

Kotah's grin makes my toes curl and a zing of horny heat hits me in the hoohaw. Both of them growl.

"Sorry. Fresh air. Let me work off some of this energy."

Brant checks the monitor that tracks movement in the driving shed above and the perimeter outside. Once he's satisfied that no bad guys are waiting to pounce on us, he presses his hand on the locking screen and opens things up.

"We should get groceries and stock the kitchen. Then I wouldn't get so hangry after hours and hours of mind-blowing sex." I smile at my mates and bite my lip. "I can't believe you two aren't ravenous after all the calisthenics."

Brant chuckles, hops into the front seat of the golf cart, and Kotah and I slide into the second row. "Unless I miss my guess, Margo and Ben will have a brunch buffet ready for us when we arrive at the ranch. She asked me to text her half an hour before we head out. I'm sure she's almost ready for us."

I pull out my phone and call Jaxx... it goes to voicemail.

Next, I call up Hawk and try him... it goes to voicemail.

"They must be sleeping in."

Brant guns us over a rise and we bounce off the seat and get air. Kotah holds on to the frame with his left hand and wraps his right arm around my shoulder. "I'm guessing your mating with Brant had a lot to do with Jaxx and Hawk's progression in mating."

"Then I'm glad I was part of it in some way."

"Now, the question will be if Hawk's defenses are down or if it was a momentary moment of weakness."

I laugh. "We've both had sex with Jaxx. That man is addictive. No matter how stubborn Hawk is, my bet is that he can't help but want more."

Kotah chuckles and palms the front of his jeans. "Time to change the subject. We're about to sit down with Brant's family and I don't want to be noticeably aroused at the table."

Brant snorts. "Trust me. That wouldn't even register. I can't even tell you how many off-color things I've contributed to the breakfast table here."

"Do tell, Bear," I say. "I'm all ears."

*Hawk*

I roll out of bed around noon and feel almost fully back to myself. My shower is hot and quick. I towel off, brush my teeth, probe the bullet entry wound in my chest and the one at my hip, and then find my duffle on the floor by the dresser.

Jaxx is dead to the world, sprawled out naked, the sun of the day warming his ripped and sinewy physique. Fuck me he's beautiful. My first instinct is to balk and play down what went down between us. That would be a dick move.

I'm tired of always playing the dick card.

I grab my phone and take a picture. Sex with Jaxx signifies more than me being weak in a moment of heightened wanton. Sex with Jaxx marks the moment my world shifted toward believing in a future with these four.

"That's a very contemplative smile," the Jaguar says, a coy expression on his face. "You planning on blackmailing me with naked pictures?"

"A keepsake—just for me—if you don't mind. I've got encrypted security on my phone and retinal recognition. It won't go beyond my viewing."

He rolls onto his back and slides one arm under his head. The position stretches out his six-pack and looks like something you'd see on an erotic website. With his free hand, he reaches between his legs and adjusts things. "Here, take another one of my good side now that I'm awake."

I don't know what's gotten into me, but I can't say no. With his cock swelling and shifting up the ridges of his abs I fight my instincts. "If my life were my own, I would totally come back to bed."

"But?"

"But, I want to see if anyone has tracked us here, I need to check in on Calli and the others, and I also need to follow up with Lukas on the missing teens and a few FCO issues."

Jaxx dips his chin and strokes himself. "Suit yourself—I'm self-sufficient—but I gotta say this bad boy is your fault. Standing there aroused and naked and taking sexy pictures of me set the tone."

I glance down and curse. "It's hard enough being around Calli and keeping focused on work. Now I've got you to tempt me too."

Jaxx swings around and crawls to the end of the bed. He sits, with his feet on the floor, and spreads his knees. "Come here for a sec before you have to go."

"I recognize that look, Jaxx. If I come over there, we're never getting out of this room."

His smile is all sultry feline. "I promise. My cat just wants a drink of cream, then I'll let you leave."

My cock bobs against my belly and I curse my lack of self-control. I hold up my finger. "And then I leave."

He trails his finger over his heart and makes a cross. "As your mate, I think it's in your best interest to start every day with a brojob."

I bark a laugh. "You didn't say that."

He lets off a seductive purr and I groan and sway toward him. "Okay, we make it quick."

"I promise. I'll make you come hard and fast." He drops to his knees and points to the chair he was sitting in last night. "Sit and let me suck on you."

That ring of his alpha sends shivers through me and I'm helpless but to obey. I sit and he curls over my lap and closes the distance between his mouth and my cock. The wet heat of his mouth, the hollowing of his cheeks, his fingers gripping my sac underneath… "Oh, fuck that's too good."

Jaxx has talents I never imagined and in minutes, I'm panting. Then he starts to purr. The vibration of his animal's pleasure vacillates around my shaft and I grip the arms of the chair. My balls are tingling and the pressure is building fast. I decide I don't want to be fast. I want this to last forever.

It's too late. His head is rocking over my lap and I'm too far gone to back it up.

My gaze locks on him, savoring me. He's rapt and hungry and so fucking confident in taking what he wants. His eyes open and those turquoise pools catch me watching him.

They flash. His jaguar is close to the surface and filled with sultry satisfaction.

"Oh, fuck…" I throw my head back and stiffen. An electrical storm explodes from the base of my cock.

The purring grows louder and his grip shifts to my hips. He's sucking and swallowing and the heat of cum pushes through my crown. He has me pinned in place, devouring everything I've got.

It's so hot. Cum launches out of me again and again, in wave after wave of convulsions. The tremors don't end like they always have before… they build up and roll over each other until I'm sure I'll die from the pleasure.

How can I survive this?

I realize I'm gripping his hair and fucking his mouth like a madman. My pulse is thundering in my head and my vision goes spotty. I'm going to blackout.

Jaxx stops purring and things finally slow down.

My release ebbs to its end and I can breathe again. "What the fuck was that?"

"I told you I was going to make you come hard."

I can't look at him curled in my lap right now. I'm too raw. I lift him as I stand and flop us both on the bed. With a hand on my chest, I wait until I can breathe again. "Sorry. I didn't realize I was fucking you there until I was really fucking you hard."

"Why are you sorry?"

"Well, I certainly wasn't being a gentleman about it."

Jaxx laughs and rolls onto his belly. "You be a gentleman with Calli and Kotah. You be everything else with me." With that, he props himself up on his elbows, kisses the ever-loving hell out of me, and then pushes off the bed.

Sauntering his naked ass toward the bathroom he leaves me breathless and stunned. "Go to work, Hawk. Leave a cat to jack in the shower in private."

I groan.

"You're totally picturing it, aren't you?"

"Yes."

"Good. Now go to work. I'm a male of my word—brojob and away you go."

I lay there in a daze for a few more minutes and then the shower comes on. If I give in, we'll never get out of this room. *Right. Work. Things to do.* I grab one of our towels from last night, dry things off, and grab a pair of slacks and a golf shirt from my bag.

I glance around, wondering if my kink kit is in here too or if Calli has it from when she was looking at it. Who knew I'd be wanting it on my side trip with Jaxx? In the end, it's not here, so that's likely a good thing. I need to rethink and research before I bring up kink with the jaguar.

My cock stirs behind the fabric of my slacks and I groan. Part of me hopes that this incessant need for my mates is just the mating bond aligning and it will settle over time.

The other part hopes it never ends.

"Good morning," I say to Lukas as I stride into the kitchen and beeline it for the coffee machine.

"Good afternoon," Lukas says, a smile in his voice.

I turn and peg him with a look, but he's studiously glancing at his company iPad. "There are leftovers from dinner last night in the fridge. Milo was here and made bacon and lamb lasagna and mushroom risotto."

I chuckle and pull a plate down. "He allowed us to keep leftovers? I thought that offended his chef's sensibilities."

"It does, but Jaxx batted his eyes and used his southern charm to sweet-talk him into it. He was adamant you'd want some when you felt up to it."

I turn on the oven and slide the lasagna pan inside to heat up. "That was thoughtful. I do."

"With that drawl of his and his alpha power, your jaguar's hard to say no to, I'm sure."

I take the risotto out and set it on the counter a little more aggressively than I intend. "You got something to say to me?"

Lukas holds up his palms and smiles. "Just that I'm glad your life is starting to fulfill you. You deserve every happiness. You work too hard not to reap some rewards. Not that you need me to weigh in, but I approve."

I turn and busy myself with transferring the risotto into an oven-safe dish. I don't want to discuss Jaxx with anyone. For now, I want that part of my life to be about me and him.

"Tell me what I missed over the past two days. Where are we on things? Start with office stuff. Jaxx will want to hear the update on the attack and the teens."

*Jaxx*

By the time I get cleaned up and head out to the kitchen, Hawk has the leftovers warmed and is dishing himself a plate. He gestures to the second plate and I nod. "Yeah, thanks."

"Lukas was saying that you and he have a theory on who found us in Oregon?"

While he finishes with doling out the portions, I grab cutlery and pause at the glasses. "Wine or water?"

"Wine, thanks."

"Lukas?"

"I'm good."

I grab two wine glasses down from the stem rack, the bottle of red from last night from the fridge, and head back to the other side of the marble island. "Cool. I don't want to be the only lush imbibing so early in the day."

Lukas snorts. "Seriously, you two, it's almost three o'clock. Early was hours ago... unless you're saying this is an early dinner. Then you're good to go."

I chuckle and set out our cutlery and glasses. "But doesn't your boss look better after taking a respite?"

Lukas nods. "I told him as much a few minutes ago. Now, back to our theory. Jaxx and I backed things up all the way to the roadside attack on the tour bus, to the intended helicopter crash, to blowing up of your cabin at the Bastion, to the attack at the Oregon compound."

Hawk hands me my plate and stays on the opposite side of the counter eating while standing up. I open the bottle and pour us two generous glasses of Tuscan red. "So, four attacks. Two occurred while we were on the road and we should've been off the map. And two occurred when everyone knew we were at the Prime Palace or the Bastion."

"Okay, and what did that tell you?"

"Well, we were more interested in the two where we were on the road. We rented that tour bus, so we know that wasn't what led hostiles there. Calli's existence was only known by you four, me, Jaxx's alpha, and the Fae Council."

Hawk nods. "Agreed, that's a small group of suspects."

I chuff and swallow. "That's only *one* group of suspects—the Fae Council."

Lukas nods. "It's safe to say it wasn't any of us or Jaxx's alpha, so yeah, that leaves the council. Then, the helicopter and the cabin both happened while meeting with the council and staying on council land. And then Oregon."

Hawk takes a long sip of wine and then swallows. "And? Did you tie it to the council?"

"The question was, how did the Prima know where you were? And if she knew, where'd she find out?"

"And you think it was through her dealings with the council."

I nod. "She told Kotah that she and his father are opposed to Calli opening the portal gate and uniting the realms. Think about it. If they don't want to lose their standing in our hierarchy, why should we think the Fae Council is thinking any differently?"

Lukas taps his stylus on his iPad and turns it for Hawk. "Who has the potential to lose the most if the realms unite? It's not the people. It's not even the money runners or the rebels here or the Darkside players. It's the Fae Council."

"But there are procedures in place," Hawk says. "The FCO has the power to temporarily freeze the authority of the Fae Council and the Fae Prime should something like that happen. When I set up the Fae Council, I ensured I could shut down and veto them if ever I proved they weren't acting in the best interests of the people."

I shift my empty plate to the side and lean back in my chair with my wine. "*You* could or the *CEO* of the Fae Concealment Office?"

Hawk shrugs. "One and the same. I am the CEO and I could veto them."

Lukas points at the screen. "But what if they prove that *you* aren't acting in the best interest of the fae community. What if you're discovered to be kidnapping children, wiping families, earning money through illegal arms deals and human trafficking. What if the Fae Council levels a non-confidence vote against you and freezes your authority in the FCO?"

Hawk's fork clanks on his plate as he collects the iPad. "You think they're the ones fucking with my reputation and framing me? You think it's a preemptive strike to get me out of the way so they can reign supreme?"

Lukas nods. "That's what it's looking like, yeah."

"Those dirty motherfuckers. I'm going to kill them." Rigid with fury, he sets the iPad down and leaves the room.

I glance to Lukas and he shakes his head. "Wait for it."

*"Back-stabbing mother-fuckers!"* The crash of wood and glass down the hall makes me wince.

"Bookshelf?"

Lukas nods. "Sounds like it." Another round of cursing precedes another crash. Lukas raises his finger and says, "The desk skidded across the floor and through the window wall."

*Yikes.* There's a third round of expletives and I grimace.

"It sounds like he's ripping the drywall from the studs and the pictures are smashing to the floor."

Lukas shakes his head. "No. I've heard that one before. That's the fan and light fixture being ripped out of the ceiling and smashed on the ground."

I pour myself more wine. "You're going to need to call a carpenter."

Lukas grins. "I have one on speed dial for just such occasions. He gives us a good rate because we keep him busy."

A moment later, Hawk strides back in and reclaims his spot at the kitchen island. "Don't go into the office. We need a bit of work done."

I chuckle. "Feel better?"

"Not really, no."

"You ready for the rest of it?"

He pegs me with a heated glare and arches a brow. "There's more?"

"Maybe, maybe not. You've been patched up by Fae Council doctors more than once, yeah?"

He dips his chin. "And?"

Lukas pulls a small, handheld scanning device from his bag, laying on its side on the counter. "I want to check all of you to see if you've been tagged. It's been twisting my nuts that we keep getting ambushed in remote, undisclosed locations. I want to know why."

The muscles in Hawk's jaw twitch like mad. "Do it."

# CHAPTER SIXTEEN

*Brant*

"She's breathtaking." I stare at my mate, fully transformed, and soaring twenty feet above our heads. She's managed to get air three times over the past hour and though she can't stay up there long, I couldn't be prouder.

"You're spectacular, *Chigua*," Kotah shouts. "Try to land on your feet this time. Maybe run a bit when you touch down to absorb the momentum."

She lets off a shriek, her fiery form banking left as she circles back in a wide arc before dropping lower and lower in incremental stages.

"Don't be afraid, beautiful," I say, smiling up at her. "That's what happened last time. You were too stiff when you landed. Try to relax and absorb the landing."

"Three weeks?" Margo says, staring up in awe. "Less than a month since she transitioned from a Nary human, and she can hold her form and fly?"

I nod at my den mother. "She amazes us every day. By the time we have the last two soul shards and our alignment is complete, she'll have her flight and her fire and be ready to open the portal gate to StoneHaven."

Margo curls into my side and kisses my cheek. "I'm proud of you, cub."

"Thanks, Mama."

"Here she comes." Kotah starts running as she nears the ground, falling behind but tracking her as she gets to—

"Ow," I wince as her feet touch down and she face-plants and flips end over end like she did the last time. "'Scuse me, Mama."

"Yeah, of course, baby. You go. I'll put these groceries by the skid in the shed."

"'Kay, thanks." I run to join Kotah in checking on my mate and drop to the ground beside her. "That was good, beautiful."

Kotah drops the fire blanket over her and brushes the dirt off her face and out of her hair. "Don't be discouraged, Calli. You're doing so well."

Calli sits up and huffs. "I would rather not eat dirt every time I try to land."

"Hawk will be able to help you," the wolf says. "I'm sure there are a few avian tricks he can help you with. Once he's back, I'm sure it'll be just a case of ironing out the kinks."

Calli flops onto her back and lets out a long exhale. "I have more than a few kinks I want to iron out with him."

I chuckle. "It was too bad his last playdate ended up in vibrator interruptus."

She accepts Kotah's hand and he helps her to her feet. "Yeah, too bad I transitioned into a firebird and fried the little guy and too bad Hawk ended up with two bullets in him. Are you sure he's all right? You're not keeping out of my sight because somethings not right, are you?"

"Why would you think that?" I say. "We've always been straight with you, haven't we?"

She sighs. "Yeah, sorry. I'm just cranky. I want to see him with my own eyes and reassure myself he's okay."

"He and Jaxx were having a private fuck-fest into the wee hours.

They wouldn't have been up to the hot and heavy if Hawk wasn't recovered."

She looks up at me and smiles. "Great point, Bear."

I pull her against my chest and kiss the top of her head. After picking the dirt out of my mouth, I adjust the blanket around her and smile. "Are you quitting, or do you want to go again?"

The sound of a helicopter has the three of us looking north. "Can either of you see what that bird looks like," I say, backing toward the golf cart. My last run-in with a helicopter didn't go my way. I'd rather not repeat."

Kotah's phone rings and he answers it. "Hey, where... okay, yeah, we see you. We're in a field just east of your current heading... Okay. We'll be here."

When he hangs up, Calli's all smiles. "I take it that's our helicopter?"

"Yep."

I stretch my neck from side to side but the niggling tension in my shoulders doesn't ease. "I thought they were coming tonight once nightfall could cover their travel?"

Kotah shrugs. "I don't know. Hawk just asked that we get out somewhere open so we can meet the helicopter and that all three of us be here."

"Why?" Calli asks. "That's weird."

Kotah shields his eyes and watches as the helicopter transforms from a silver speck in the distant sky to yet another sleek and expensive example of Hawk's overcompensation for being a corporate douche.

The twin-engine Eurocopter AS365 Dauphin touches down in the fallow field where we're training and Jaxx and Hawk jump out as if their asses are on fire.

My bear's growl is lost in the high-pitch whine of the beast as we run to join them. Calli throws off the blanket and leaps at Hawk, mid-run. Catching her against his chest, he secures her in his arms. Her bare legs wrap around his hips and she's sucking his face.

Jaxx grabs the discarded blanket off the ground to cover her back up and chuckles at the PDA.

"What's wrong," I shout, over the engines when we're all huddled together.

"Most urgently," Hawk says, grimacing. "Spitfire, you're burning off my clothes."

"Oops, sorry." Calli releases him from her naked koala hold and takes a step back, accepting the fire blanket. "I missed you guys."

Jaxx brushes at the dirt covering the left side of her face and the patch of her forehead that got scraped during the last landing. "Kitten, what have you been doing to yourself."

"In a minute," Hawk says, interrupting Calli's news. "I'm sorry, but this can't wait." He takes something out of the pocket of his slacks and starts passing it over Calli's head and down her neck and over her shoulders. He scans her top to bottom, front to back.

Jaxx moves in behind Calli and wraps his arms around her when Hawk moves to Kotah. "We figured out the Fae Council chipped Hawk and think that's how they've been tracking us for the attacks."

Kotah frowns, just as the device starts beeping and its green light flips red. "What does that mean?"

"It means they've tagged you too, Wolf," Hawk says, finishing his sweep of the kid. "Jaxx, would you mind doing the honors. Kotah, take off your shirt so he can cut the chip out of you. If it's like mine, it's just below the surface."

Jaxx shifts behind Kotah and waits until his shirt is over his head. "Why have I been chipped?"

"To always know where you are, I'd guess."

Jaxx angles himself with his hands poised and releases his wicked-sharp claws to extend beyond the nailbed of his fingers. With the razor edge and his paramedic experience, the cut and removal of the little tracking device are finished with surgical precision.

Hawk moves to me next and I hold my arms out to the side and let him do his thing. "And you think it's the Fae Council behind this?"

Hawk finishes checking me over and nods. "We do. Jaxx, get rid of that."

Jaxx jogs back over to the helicopter and leans in to hand off the tracking chip. When he comes back, he's all smiles. "Lukas is going to fly back to Oregon, check Doc and Keyla, and then mail the tracking chips to the North Pole post office in Alaska. That should keep them off our backs for a bit."

Kotah stiffens. "You think they've chipped Keyla too? Then I want to go. If she's in danger…"

"I don't think she is," Hawk says. "They're keeping tabs on key players they've had access to. We don't even know that your sister is chipped. Lukas will get to her within the hour and he'll report back. Don't panic."

The helicopter takes off again and the world grows silent once more. The five of us are standing in a field and my skin is crawling. "If they know Kotah's here, they know it's probable that we're all here."

Hawk nods. "Agreed, but it's late and you vouch for the security of this bunker, so we're going to stay put for now and run through our options until we hear back from Lukas. We'll need supplies."

"That's covered," I say. "Groceries are waiting at the hatch for us to take down when we finish training."

Calli frowns. "Well, I guess that's now. I'll have to learn to land another day."

"Aw… kitten," Jaxx says, checking out her injury again. "Is that what this is?"

She sighs. "I face-plant ever time, puss. I'm hoping Hawk has a few insider bird tips for me. I'm no longer breaking my bones, but I'm a hot mess on the landing."

Hawk gestures for us to get moving and wraps an arm around her. "I've got you, Spitfire. Consider yourself safe from further face-planting. I'll get you sorted and soaring as soon as it's safe."

*Calli*

Jaxx and Hawk give us the low-down on everything they think and know. I should be more upset. I'm not. I can't help it. Yes, it sucks that Hawk and Kotah were chipped. That's a violation. And yes, I think it's awful that whoever is behind it is trying to smear Hawk out of the company he built so they can keep the status quo.

"Yes, it's awful, but we shouldn't let it freak us out," I say to four disbelieving mates. "Big picture here, boys. We're on to them. Our quint is fully mated. And if I continue getting stronger, I'm going to open that portal gate whether they like it or not."

"Hells yeah, you are, beautiful," Brant says. "In the meantime, we're safe, we know what we're looking for now, and we're off their radar."

Hawk nods. "I give it two or three days before they figure out that the chips are in a post office earmarked for Santa. In that time, we've got to figure out who we can trust at FCO, find the rest of the teens, figure out if it's the whole Fae Council that's rotten or just some, and plan our counter-attack."

Jaxx is pulling out liquor bottles and lining them up on the kitchen counter next to the blender. "It's to our advantage that Calli is burning through the stages of her transition so freakin' fast. There's no way they can be expecting her to be able to call her phoenix forth and flying yet."

Hawk frowns. "Well, that's not exactly true. I've been giving the council regular status reports."

Brant curses and throws him a dirty look. "Of course, you have. Did you think that maybe it was none of their business and you should keep Calli's personal deets private?"

"No," I say, getting snippy. "It's Hawk's job to be on top of things that affect the realm. We all thought the council was on our side. They've been encouraging our alignment since the beginning. Don't peg their betrayal on him."

"She's right, Bear," Jaxx says, setting up the blender. "We're looking at high-level corruption tainting people we all know personally. My feline Prime, Dane, is a god to our species. Kotah's parents... yeah, they are asshole parents, but they're respected as treasured leaders...

Hawk is friends with every person on that council and they chose to discredit him."

Jaxx tips a bottle of tequila for a long pour over a couple of cups of ice and cuts a few limes. "Tonight, we devolve into Margarita madness. Tomorrow we formulate a plan."

Brant frowns. "Really? You think Margarita madness is a good idea?"

He splashes in some orange liqueur and smiles. "No. It's a great idea. Hawk missed out on the last one and we're all talked out for one day. When life screws you, you drink and regroup."

"That's poetic," I say.

"Thank you, kitten. Now, explain the rules to the noob while I set us up. Kotah, get the table ready, if you will. Brant, clear the deck."

Brant shakes his head but gets up, grabs the red solo cups, and sets his chair and Jaxx's over by the door. Kotah puts his chair away too, and when Hawk and I stand, Brant takes those too.

I crack my knuckles and giggle at the look on Hawk's face. "Okay, so, we all stand around the table. Jaxx pours each of us four cups of margaritas. A four-ounce cup, a three-ounce cup, a two-ounce cup, and one with one ounce. The game is to drink them and then flip the empty cup from sitting on it's base at the edge of the table upside down, like this." I take an empty cup and demonstrate.

Kotah chuckles. "You're supposed to do one at a time but Calli likes to drink all of hers first and then flip them all."

"It's a strategy, Wolf. And might I say, I kicked your sweet and sexy ass."

Hawk chuckles. "And this is the occasion when I found you in your underwear vomiting into a kitchen sink and the men all naked?"

I smile. "Yeah, because we raised the stakes and I won. The first person to drink and flip gets to call the game for that round as well as his or her opponent. At the palace, we had a ping-pong table and played quarters on the other table. Here, we have an entire game room, so there's no end to choices."

"And the naked part?"

"The loser of the chosen game has to take a layer off before the next round."

"It's hardly high-concept. You'll catch on," Jaxx says, coming over with the booze. He pours out our starter rounds and takes one cup from my pile. "Tonight, you get one cup less, kitten. I don't want you sick like that again."

I laugh and rub my hands together. "My evil plan is working. Give the female an advantage."

He chuckles and adds my cup to Brant's row. "And you get an extra cup. We should've taken body mass into account last time."

Brant chuckles and cracks his knuckles. "Whatever, Jaguar. It's not going to help you."

When we're all set, Jaxx sets the egg timer on the stove and we all stand ready. "When the timer buzzes, we go."

The five of us stand hands at the ready and knees bent like we were awaiting the starter's gun for an Olympic event.

*Bzzzzz*

"Go!"

We're hours into the madness when my world starts to get spinny and I think about tapping out. Jaxx must sense my state because he wraps an arm around my hip and has me say goodnight to Hawk and Kotah facing off at the air hockey table. I look around for Brant, but I think he went to pee.

It's the first alone time with Jaxx I've had and my curiosity is burning hot in my core. "Okay, I'm dying," I say, snuggling into him. My footwork is sloppy, but the world is still floating in a fun whirl around me, so I'm good. "I tried to play it all cool because obvi that's the way you two are playing it but spill. You and Hawk. What happened?"

Jaxx flashes me that crooked smile of his and I'm horny just imagining it. "I told you before, kitten, a southern gentleman doesn't kiss and tell."

I roll my eyes and shake my head. Woops, too much…

I tip and Jaxx chuckles and scoops me up in his arms. I sigh and press my cheek to his chest. Jaxx is always so steady and he smells *soooo* good and I'm really quite drunk.

"I missed you, puss." I say before I remember what I was asking him about. "Hawk's one of ours. Can't I know?"

He sets me on the king bed that Brant, Kotah, and I used last night and reaches between my legs. The snap of cotton and silk represents the murder of the crotch of my undies. "Hey, cheating. I haven't lost them yet."

"And you're still wearing them, they're just modified." He spreads my knees, gives me a testing lick, and then crawls up my body sliding his stiff cock inside me. "I missed you too, baby."

I groan and wrap my elbows around his neck while the world spins. "I wanna know about you and Hawk."

"You know," he whispers next to my ear as he establishes as slow invade and retreat. "You feel it on the mating bond and it's blatantly in our scents. Hawk and I mated. You know all you need to."

My arms are heavy, so I let them flop onto the mattress and simply absorb. "You're mean."

He stops moving. "Really? I thought I was being sweet and making love to my mate."

I whimper and sigh. "Fine. You are. I'm just sad you won't give me the dirty deets."

He chuckles and gets back to loving me. "When he's ready to share, how about we show you. The voyeur in you would like that, wouldn't you? Do you want a front-row view of Hawk and I naked and going at it?"

I groan and wrap my legs around his thighs, feeling the dreamy drunkenness of the night taking hold. "Yes, I do."

"Good. Now focus on the mate who's currently fucking you. He needs your attention. My mate was taken, and my cat has been pacing for days. I need you, Calli. Let me love you."

# CHAPTER SEVENTEEN

Hawk

$\mathcal{I}$'m up, showered, and enjoying my second cup of coffee when Calli strides into the kitchen looking as bright-eyed as ever in yoga pants, a sleeveless tank top, and her copper-streaked, golden hair pulled back in a ponytail. It blows my mind sometimes at how down to earth she is. Makeup is only for the biggest of occasions, fine clothing, and jewelry the same. She's happiest to hang out in sweats, eat frozen appetizers, and play flip cup with her mates.

I've never known anyone quite like her.

There are no hidden agendas with her. No deceptions. If she wants or expects something, she speaks her mind. And if she's upset about something, you don't have to guess what it is, you'll know.

Today, she's happy. And seeing her happy makes me happier than I ever expected. "Nice to see your phoenix healing took care of any hangover you should be suffering."

She giggles and grabs a mug from the rack. "Honestly, next to being a mythical firebird that can fly—well, almost fly—and having four incredible, sex-god males crazy for me—and each other—the no hangover thing is one of my favorite perks."

I smile at the not-so-subtle 'and each other' and take the bait. "And what do you think about me and Jaxx?"

She beams and practically bounces over to where I'm perched on a breakfast stool. "I think it's awesome and hot and Jaxx says when you two are comfortable, I can watch."

"He did, did he? You two discussed our private time?" I sigh, disappointed in the trust I placed that he'd keep our liaison between us.

"No. Don't do that." She strokes the tension of my brow with her thumb, looking sad. "He refused to tell me anything good. All he said was that you mated—which I knew—and that anything that happened was behind closed doors and private. When I whined and persisted, he said maybe one day I could join you. Don't be mad at Jaxx. He kept your private stuff private."

I draw a steadying breath, surprised at how vulnerable trusting in these new relationships makes me feel. For a guy who never needed anyone, it's weird to care what people say and do.

Calli still looks worried.

My mug *clinks* on the marble counter and turn on my stool to face her. "Okay, I'm not upset with Jaxx. I asked that he not discuss what happened because I want time to process. It's important to me that he respects that."

"He does. And I won't push him anymore, I promise."

The loss of her cheery smile from a moment ago hurts. "I'm sorry. I'm not good at any of this yet… but I'm trying. Please find your smile again."

She leans forward and hugs me. "I think you're doing great. I'll try to mind my own and be patient."

I chuckle at the impossibility of that. "So, you're looking forward to watching Jaxx and I, are you?"

And just like that, her smile is back, and her eyes are alight and beaming. "Mhmm, yes please."

I cup her jaw and capture her lips. Kissing my mate is like a system reboot. All my programs and apps update and I feel stronger and better prepared to face the bombardment of the world. She steps between my knees and deepens the kiss, reminding me the two of us have unfinished business with a certain kink kit.

When she eases back, I pinch her chin and steal another quick kiss. "I've been off-balance since you were taken. I need some private time with you soon."

"If you didn't insist on sleeping alone, we might've already taken care of that."

I shake my head. "With the amount of alcohol I consumed last night, I couldn't take my pills. I didn't want to take the chance of hurting you again."

She presses a kiss on my cheek. "You didn't hurt me. And, whenever you're ready, I'm willing. Just give me the signal. Honestly, the possessive mate madness after I got back has been fun. Kinda the silver lining to getting highjacked."

The coffeemaker clicks off and I gesture for her to go get herself sorted. "There's no silver lining to you getting highjacked. If you want more sex, that can be arranged."

Jaxx laughs as he comes into the kitchen. "Boy, did I time that right. You want more sex, kitten? I'm with Hawk. That can be arranged."

She rolls her eyes, grabs her coffee, a bowl, and a box of kid's cereal, and settles on the stool beside me. "Not what I meant. I was saying my kidnapping brought out an aggressive need in you four to assert yourselves sexually with me. I've enjoyed it."

I pass her the milk. "Then consider yourself on notice for some more sexual assertion. My alpha side is growing quite demanding and I won't be able to stave it off much longer."

Jaxx arches a brow and throws me a look.

And just like that, I want not only to ravish Calli but to be ravished by Jaxx.

Calli holds up her spoon and points from me to Jaxx and back again. "Whoa, did the sexual tension in the room just redline, or is it just me?"

"Eat your cereal, kitten," Jaxx says, pointing to her bowl. "You need to build up your strength for your firebird session this afternoon. No more crashing and burning."

"Oh," Calli says, crunching her cereal fast and swallowing. "I kinda burned up a farmer's field and single-handedly ruined his yield this year. I promised him my husband would be happy to pay market value for the damaged crop. I hope you don't mind."

"Your husband, am I?" I like the sound of that and it gives me an idea about something I've neglected to source out and buy for us. "Well, as it happens, your husband has very deep pockets and is happy to support a local farmer."

Jaxx slips a flavor pod into the coffeemaker and grabs a fruit pastry. "How does that saying go… In winter chill and summer heat, farmers and ranchers work so we eat."

I point at the colored junk Calli's putting into her system and frown. "No farmer grew that. Let's get something more wholesome in you."

"Kotah's out for a morning run."

I snort. "He's wholesome, true, but that's not what I meant and you know it. Jaxx, are you up for a round of your Texas westerns?"

Jaxx waggles his brow and grabs a carton of eggs from the fridge. "Coming right up."

*Brant*

I'm sweeping up in the driving shed, waiting for Kotah to return from his morning run when my phone rings. I check the ID and smile. "Hannah, tell me you've got good news."

The line hangs empty and I check the screen to make sure the call didn't drop. "Hannah? You there? Are you ass-dialing me?"

There's a noise in the background that I can't quite make out and I strain to hear it. My skin is crawling, and I drop my arm to open the security app Hawk added to all our phones. I begin a record and trace.

Kotah trots in through the shed door on all fours with his tongue hanging out. He looks relaxed and I hold up my fingers and beckon him closer. "Can you hear what's happening in the background here, Wolf?"

Wildling hearing is far more acute in our animal forms and the wolf cocks his head to one side. We both stay like that, listening to the faint background noises until the phone beeps and the call ends.

Kotah shifts and stands before me looking puzzled. "What was that about?"

"I don't know. Hannah called but never said anything. I don't know if it was an accident or a call for help."

"I think it might be a bit of both. It sounded to me like she was surveying something and couldn't or wasn't saying anything to you. Her breathing didn't sound panicked, but she was definitely observing someone in distress. I could hear them softly whimpering in the distance."

I frown and open the rusted-out electrical panel to access the hand scanner. "Access, Brantley Robbins, granted."

The motor beneath the skid of manure hums to life and slides things to the side so we can access the hatch. I open things up and gesture for Kotah to start down.

"I put a trace on it. Hopefully, Hawk's fancy gadgets are as good as he boasts. Enough of this planning bullshit. We need to get the others mobile and *do* something."

With my bear growing more agitated by the moment, I find Jaxx playing pool solo in the game room.

"Where are Calli and Hawk?"

Jaxx looks up from the line of his cue and smiles. "Resetting his animal side. They haven't had much alone time and he's losing his hold."

"I gotta talk to him. We need to get moving."

"Problem?"

"Maybe." I fill Jaxx in on Hannah's phone call and he frowns. "You tracked it, though, yeah?"

I nod. "Yeah, but I need him to tell me where she is."

"Okay, then we'll call Lukas to send the helicopter for us and start packing up. We'll leave Calli and Hawk to their fun for now and then we'll catch them up."

"Jaxx, kids are missing, and teams are out there putting themselves in danger. That's more important than him polishing his rocks. We need to address the shit that's hitting us from all directions. I'm breaking things up."

Jaxx straightens, his eyes flashing with the strength of his alpha. "No, you're not, Bear. After Calli was reclaimed you and she spent the next twelve hours on and off one another. Hawk's had one private moment with her—*one*—and that was over a week ago and before she was kidnapped. There's nothin' either of them can do that we can't handle, and it'll take an hour for the helicopter to get here. Leave them be."

I chuff. "I get that you're flying the flag for team avian now that you and he crossed swords but—"

Jaxx pounces over the table in a blur, the roar of his cat echoing as he comes. My ass hits the floor a split-second before my head clunks on the concrete and I'm seeing stars. Straddling my chest, he presses the pool cue against my throat. I work for oxygen as he leans close and bares his teeth.

"Talk to me like that again, Bear. I dare you."

Fuck, his eyes are lit like neon. He pegs me with a hostile glare, and I can't fight biology. I drop my gaze and turn my head to expose my neck. He's alpha. I'm beta. No matter how relaxed he usually is about the whole dominance thing, biology rules.

"Listen carefully," he says, his voice laced with a growl, "and let this sink way down deep. Spout off about meaningless shit and I'll let you have your fun. Belittle our mates or the relationships we're buildin' and we have a problem. Hawk is one of us and we're becomin' a family. Show some fuckin' respect."

I bite my tongue and let off a long sigh. "You're right. I get mouthy when I'm frustrated. I'm sorry."

He searches the sincerity of my apology before he peels off. "Think before you speak, Bear. We need to build our mating bonds, not tear at them. Sincerity goes a lot further than sarcasm."

Sitting up, I rub the back of my head and wince when I prod an egg swelling up. "Not my best event... but I'll try."

He's still pissed. I read it in the tension of his coiled muscles and the slight sneer of his lip.

I get to my feet and hold out my arms. "If it helps, take a shot at me. This isn't the first time I've pissed off someone I care about. They always seem to feel better after a good, old-fashioned punch to the face."

Jaxx rolls his eyes. "I'll pass—"

Movement in my periphery has me turning my head. Kotah's fist comes out of nowhere. The kid has a wicked left hook and my head snaps back. I stagger back and steady myself on the side of the pool table.

Damn, I can't feel my face.

Warmth drips down my chin and I probe the split lip. "All right. Are we good—"

The follow-up right cross sails into view and connects just under the orbital bone of my eye. Fuck. The kid might be half my size, but he's been training in offensive and defensive fighting since he was a pup and has fists of concrete.

Kotah shakes his fist and I blink down at him while my hamster drags its fuzzy ass back into its wheel. "Was that for Jaxx or something I did to you?"

"Both. And you're right. I do feel better."

I chuckle and stretch my jaw from side to side. "Yay, you. Do you mind explaining? Did you save that up or was it spontaneous? Am I clueless? I thought we were good."

He stares at me a heart-achingly long time before he leans against the wall and crosses his ankles. "Mostly spontaneous... but you deserved it."

I laugh. "No argument, though technically, I offered the shot to Jaxx."

"Same offense," Kotah says. "My entire life, I've been judged and told I don't measure up. In this mating, I found a place where I'm free of that, safe to be loved and admired for the man I am. Sniping Jaxx about something private he shared with Hawk hurts me too. It makes me wonder if I *am* safe from opinion and harsh comments."

Inwardly, I curse my stupid self. "You're safe, Wolf. I need to rein it in. Bears talk shit more than most. A cutting jibe to us is fun with friends. I burned more than a few bridges when I started with the FCO and couldn't figure out why people were so touchy. It's a species thing, I suppose, but Jaxx is right. We're building bonds here not tearing at them. I apologize if I upset you."

The kid's easy smile returns, and I can breathe again. "Good, because I, for one, love crossing swords with Jaxx and didn't want you to ruin it for me."

Jaxx arches a brow and smiles. "Anytime, my man. And now that our self-proclaimed meathead has mated with Calli maybe he'll participate more in the horizontal hijinx."

"Yeah, I will," I say, considering the options. "It's too bad we're on our way out. I can think of a couple of things we've yet to try."

# CHAPTER EIGHTEEN

Jaxx

*I*t takes ten minutes to call Lukas, ask him to track the location of Brant's call, and get the ball rolling on the helicopter. When I've got things locked down, I tell Kotah to pack up the perishables and I leave him to go update Calli and Hawk. I listen at the bedroom door for a few seconds before I knock. "Is it safe to enter?" *Or better yet, join?*

"Yeah," Hawk says.

I let myself into the bedroom Hawk slept in last night and smile at our girl snuggled in and draped over our avian mate looking sated. I considered snuggling the man myself after we collapsed this morning but didn't want to push my luck not knowing if he'd appreciate it.

Note to self. He looks quite content.

Hawk chuckles. "Did you interrupt for a reason or just to get a visual?"

I bite my bottom lip and rub a hand over my awakening cock. "While I won't deny the visual is good for my soul, no, I'm here because we're readying to move." I fill them in on the call from Hannah and what Kotah heard in the background. I mention that

146

Brant is quite worked up about it but omit our little Come to Jaguar moment in the game room.

I'm almost finished the update when a call rings in on Hawk's computer. Our cellphone signal is spotty in the bunker but plugging into a landline works fine.

Being the closest to the desk, I glance over and read the icon that pops up. "Lukas is hailing you for a video chat."

"What now?" Hawk frowns and swaggers over to open the call. "You said he's sending the chopper, right?"

I toss him his shirt and he pulls it on before sitting at the desk. He's still nakey on the bottom half, but only we know that. "I asked him to. Maybe he wants to double-check with you." I step in behind him to shield any view of Calli in the bed and nod to Lukas when the line connects.

"What's wrong?" Hawk snaps.

Lukas doesn't seem bothered by the tone, either that or he's so used to it he doesn't notice it. "Keyla is on a call with her mother in the other room. The Prime has taken a turn. She and Kotah are being called to the palace."

"Fuck," Hawk says. "Is the helicopter on its way?"

"It left five minutes ago. You've got about forty-five until it's at your door."

"Okay, we'll meet you at the airstrip in Oregon in two hours, give or take. Ready the plane to go to Kansas with everyone except you, Brant, and I. We will handle team two and what they found. Have you tracked where they are?"

"Down the Pacific Coast Highway in Northern California. I haven't made contact yet, but I'm trying."

"Okay, we'll see where we are when we arrive."

"Understood."

When the video call drops, Calli hops up and jogs into the bathroom. "Give me ten."

Hawk gets up from the desk and I toss his slacks from where they drape over the dresser. "I've been thinking a lot about why the universe put us together and the past couple of weeks. We've been getting hit on all sides and reacting, but I feel like we're missing something important."

"Like what?"

"Like that we're sheep being herded toward the slaughter. Someone's pulling our strings and we're too distracted by the bombs going off around us to see through the smoke."

"Okay, what do we need to do to become proactive?"

"I think divide and conquer is unavoidable."

"I don't want to divide," Calli says from the bathroom as the shower comes on. "I hate divide."

"No more than the rest of us, kitten."

Hawk pulls his pants on commando and frowns. "Trust me, Spitfire, I'd rather hunker down in here for the next year and live off champagne and orgasms, but with the world in the state it is, we need to get control of the clusterfuck that is our life. Divide and conquer is unavoidable."

"Do you think that's why the Fae Council has been pushing for us to drop off the map and align the quint? Are they trying to keep us from noticing what's happening?"

Hawk frowns. "It would serve their purpose if we did."

Another knock brings Kotah into the mix. "I've got us packed up, the groceries bagged, and our linens stripped. I'd like to do Margo and Ben the courtesy of leaving the place in the same condition as we found it. Can I get your sheets to start the laundry?"

"That's thoughtful, sweet prince," Calli says, hustling out with a towel wrapped under her arms. "Tell Brant I'd like to ride up to the main house with him to drop off the supplies and thank his family for their hospitality. Just give me a second to throw on some clothes."

The three of us get distracted watching Calli whip off her towel and bend for her discarded clothes. Our sexy phoenix doesn't seem to realize the X-rated show she's flashing us, so no one lets on. I meet Hawk's smile and try to focus. "Kotah, we have some bad news, buddy."

Hawk nods. "I just got a call, Wolf. Keyla's speaking with your mother. We don't have any specifics, but we were told that your father has taken a turn and you two need to get back to the palace."

He stiffens and the smile drains from his face.

"I'm sorry, sugar," Calli says, coming in for a hug. "No matter what the man may or may not mean to you, him doing poorly hurts you and your plans. Just know that we're all here for you and you won't face any of it solo."

"What she said." I squeeze his arm and offer him a smile. "You're ours and we're a package deal. We got you."

Hawk nods. "Calli and Jaxx will return to the palace with you. There, with Doc and Keyla's help, you five will tend to your Prime duties and start digging into the Fae Council and what we're missing. Brant and I will go with Lukas to wherever Hannah and team two were working to track down the next cell of gifted kids."

Kotah casts me a pinched look and I couldn't agree more. "You and Brant? Is that the best pairing if we want to get things done quickly?"

Hawk shrugs. "Why not? We've been working fairly well together recently. Am I missing something?"

"Nothing to write home about," Brant says, joining the crowd. "We're all mates, right? All for one and one for all."

The look he gives me is a solid reassurance that my message from earlier hit home. "We are."

He nods. "And for sure, Hawk and I can spend a few days together without killing one another. Who knows, he might even start appreciating my charm and want to ravish me like he did you, Jaxx."

I bark a laugh. "In your dreams, Bear."

"Not bloody likely," Hawk says, but there's no heat in his comment. "I've got my hands full for now."

The look he throws me is a hot invitation for another go with me. "Sharpie me in on your dance card, avian. At your earliest convenience, we're on."

He waggles his brow and offers one of the first, genuine smiles I've seen outside the bedroom.

"That's so hot," Calli says.

"Back to the planning," Brant says. "I'm not keen on Calli being at the palace when we know there are council spies and sympathizers afoot."

"You mean my parents," Kotah says. "No need to sugarcoat it, Bear. My parents stand in direct opposition to us opening the gate. Well, the good news is my father might be dead by the time we get there. Problem solved."

Calli hugs him again. "No one wants that, Wolf. Life is complicated, sure, but parents are a tricky subject. None of us wants him dead."

"True story," I say, tugging on his braid. "None of us wants you thrown into whatever chaos is in store for you either. It's not like that."

Hawk shifts next to Kotah and bends to look directly into his eyes. "The truth is we don't know how deep their opposition goes. Maybe they aren't part of the larger plot to keep Calli from opening the portal gate and just wanted to control you enough to keep things status quo."

Kotah sighs. "Yeah, maybe they're only worried about our standing and staying in power regardless of what's best for the two realms of the fae. That's much better."

Hawk puts an arm around Kotah and hugs him to his side. When he kisses the side of his head, a schoolboy flicker of excitement bursts with hope in my chest.

Go, Hawk!

You've got this, my man.

"You can't pick your parents, Wolf," he says. "Look at my sitch. Sabastian Barron Whitehouse the fourth—a.k.a. Daddy Dearest—is one of the most power-hungry consumers of light and goodness you've ever had the pleasure of not knowing. I wouldn't be surprised if he's one of the alumni board of Darkside and plotting to kill us all right now."

"Nice," Brant says. "Maybe it's not so bad to grow up not knowing your parents."

Calli shrugs. "I'm sure they can't all be nightmares. Mine were great while I had them, and look at the Stantons. Jaxx's mom and dad are awesomesauce."

*Yes, they are.* I never realized how blessed Laney and I were until looking at my life through the eyes of my mates. "Then it's settled. No matter what happens, you guys can adopt my parents as your own. They'll be over the moon and you'll never need anyone else."

Calli frowns at Brant and points at his face. "Your lip is bleeding... and are you getting a shiner?"

He pats his lip and nods. "Yeah. And one hell of a goose egg on the back of my head. Fuck you very much, Jaxx."

"Hey, don't talk the talk and you won't walk the walk."

Calli frowns at me. "You punched him in the face?"

"No," Kotah says, grinning. "That was me. Jaxx knocked him on the floor and choked him with a pool cue."

Calli looks from Brant to me to Kotah and then back to Brant. "What the hell happened?"

I shrug. "Just ironing out a few mating wrinkles. Nothing to be concerned about."

Except Calli looks very concerned.

Brant puts up his hands in surrender. "I was an asshole and my mates helped me see the error of my ways."

"You're welcome," Kotah says.

Hawk arches a brow. "By Jaxx's comment about us working together, I assume I was the point of contention."

"Bear, seriously?" Calli says, looking crushed. "I thought we were past that. It hurts all of us when you talk shit about Hawk."

Brant smiles and points to his split lip. "That was explained to me quite succinctly. And hey, with a thick skull like mine, sometimes you gotta pound it in there. Message received. S'all good."

"Are you sure?"

He flashes us a saucy smile and steps up to Hawk. The look of trepidation on the avian's face is mirrored around the room. Brant meets him chest to chest and slaps his back. "This is me apologizing for all the shit. You rubbed me the wrong way from the get-go and I decided right then who you were. That was shitty and unfair."

Hawk lips narrow and I'm not sure what he's thinking. "Luckily, stupidity isn't a crime, so you're free to make amends. Apology accepted. I'm certainly not one to judge talking shit and upsetting people. I do, however, sincerely hope you'll stop painting me as the root of all evil."

Brant eases back a little and waggles his brow. "How about a kiss to seal the deal."

Hawk shoves him away. "In your dreams."

"Too soon?"

Calli shakes her head. "So, they punch you and choke you and that makes you want to kiss him? Does that make any sense to anyone?"

The four of us all shrug and nod.

"Men."

I laugh. "Go, team."

~

*Brant*

I pack my duffle and track Kotah's scent down the tunnel. Below the hatch, I find him leaning against the wall beside the ladder. His arms are crossed, and his head is down. I don't have to possess the empathic sensitivity of an Omega to know he's upset and hurting.

"Wolf? You okay? Anything I can do?"

He doesn't bother to look at me. "No. It takes a lot out of me to know I have to go back there. I despise the palace. My father thought sending me away was punishment for me not conforming to his mold, but the joke was on him. When I was at university, I could breathe for the first time in my life."

"I don't blame you for not wanting to go back. I wish I could be there to help you through—" The mixture of emotion in his eyes guts me. "What?"

"I'm sorry too. I blindsided you. It felt good at the time, but I don't want my fists to be our parting interaction."

I drop my duffle at my feet and face him straight on. "We're fine. I deserved it. In fact, I think I should apologize a bit more."

"You don't have to."

"I want to." I step in tight and claim his lips. Kotah's mouth is always so soft, his kiss so gentle. Connecting with him sears my soul… Every. Damn. Time.

With our kiss in play, I run a hand down the front of his pants and find the latch of his fly. I pop the button and open things up, easing back from his mouth. "It occurs to me that though you made it clear you're willing, I haven't taken the opportunity to let you know how special you are to me. That's bad form. I'm sorry."

"Do we have time?"

"We make time." I drop both hands to work his pants and boxers down his thighs. "I don't want you sad about punching me to be our last encounter either. Consider this my attempt to take some of the edges off returning to the palace."

"What about you?"

He reaches for the tab of my jeans, and grab his wrists and drop to one knee. "No, Wolf. This is about you this time. All you."

The smile that earns me lights up my insides. It also makes me realize how little the kid takes for himself. He's the giver of the quint. He deserves to have moments of us being devoted to him to fill his Omega wellsprings.

The skin of the wolf's navel is hot silk under my lips. I pay homage to the area while stoking up his anticipation. It's not just him, I'm winding up. Everything about this has my mighty pulse pumping against the fly of my jeans. My body is jonesing for what Kotah offered, despite my hesitation.

But no, this is for him.

I lick my lips, part my mouth, and sink over the weeping crown of his cock. I hiss as the richness of his essence floods my mouth. Why the hell didn't I know what he tastes like? The times we've been together things been wildly out of control and with others involved.

This time is different.

This time, I'm not here to get my rocks off. This is about new beginnings and enjoying every sensual nuance. I file every groan, every brush of the wolf's fingers through my hair, every ounce of lust and devotion in the air into my memory.

Later, when we're lonely and far apart, I'll pull them out and warm myself. Maybe he will too.

In our few encounters, we've never paired off. It's always been a frenzy of friction between us, Jaxx, and Calli. Too much hunger to register where hands were or who rubbed what or to take it all in.

This is something else. This is more.

I growl as his hips rock and he fucks my mouth. He's come so far in his confidence. It's been an honor to witness him blossom. I let my bear prowl forward and as much as I wanted this to be a simple gift of affection, my yearning to mount him and mate him is about biological need.

"Fuck, I want you, Wolf," I gasp, sucking off his engorged crown. "I want you to be mine. All mine."

His eyes roll back in his head and his legs shudder in my grip. "I want that... so much."

On a hard yank, I undo the front of my jeans and set my cock free. Pushing him back against the wall, I grind our bellies so our hard cocks rub together between us.

We both curse, in the best possible way.

Despite my spouting off about Jaxx and Hawk, nothing about two of us could ever be wrong. Not the skin-on-skin, the friction of our erections rubbing, or the frenzy of the wet heat of our mouths consuming one another.

Dizzy from the blood pounding through my body, I am truly a happy man. Pleasure rushes at me from every angle.

With a quick shift, I break away and bend to unzip my duffle. I grab the bottle of lube I picked up after our first play session and stop to stare at our wolf.

"Fuck, you're perfect."

Kotah's brow comes down hard, but there's no changing it. He's a beautifully made male, fit and graceful, with the royal choker of his standing banding his throat and the most gorgeous mane of chestnut hair. "What's wrong?" Kotah asks. "Did you change your mind about mating me?"

"Yes and no," I say, offering him the bottle. "Will you do the honors?"

He accepts the bottle and his head cants to the side. "You want me to lube you up?"

I shake my head. "I want you to claim me. The way I figure it, Hawk is alpha and will top you during your claiming as Jaxx did. Do you want to take instead of being taken?"

The grin that breaks across his face says I finally got something right today. "You don't mind?"

"You fucking me to complete our bonding? Hells no, I'm looking forward to it. I wish we were somewhere nicer for you, though. This tunnel isn't that—"

The world tilts as I get spun and throw my palms against the wall to keep my face from getting mashed into the concrete. No, the world is fine. Kotah's just accepting my invitation... quite earnestly, I might add.

I get with the program fast and push my jeans down further and widen my stance. The sound of lube squeezing free from the bottle precedes Kotah putting that moisture to good use, and a moment later, he's pressed up behind me. . .

"You're sure I take the honors?"

"Please," I gasp, desperation in my voice.

It strikes me that this is maybe the most vulnerable I've ever been with another man—maybe another person.

Raw and honest.

Kotah reaches around my hip and grips my cock as he lines up. He doesn't waste time with a preamble. He eases past the resistance and then thrusts inside with a lightning-fast strike. I nearly come right then. Planting my palms wider, I brace myself for what is coming.

The throaty growl of my bear echoes off the hard surfaces and I'm sure is heard throughout the bunker. If the others didn't sense our fucking around from the mating bond, they know about it now.

I don't care.

This is Kotah's moment as much as it is mine and I want him to claim every bit of power he needs to move forward in the days to come. His hips thrust and retreat and every grunt and groan gets me hotter.

He lets go of my cock and then one hand on my hip and the other in my hair. My breath escapes as my head snaps back, and my wolf uses his newfound leverage to keep pumping, pumping, pumping . . .

My skull tingles from his fierce grip and I adjust my feet. I widen my stance so he can get inside me as hard and as deep as possible. The sensation has me gasping for breath, panting for more, my balls burning with the need to explode.

"You're mine, Bear," he growls, behind me. "I'm laying my claim. Now and forever."

He punctuates his point by reaching around my hips and reclaiming my cock. The connection is too much, too hot. I let off a shout, and Kotah comes right along with me. We orgasm together, our throaty grunts all-male ecstasy.

Kotah rides out his tremors and collapses against my back. When he catches his breath, he laughs. "Yeah, maybe this would've been easier in one of the bedrooms."

I shrug. "I think we did fine." I pull a dirty shirt out of my bag and do the honors of cleaning both of us off. When our clothes are back in place and things are properly put away, I pull him against my chest for a kiss. "Thanks. That'll be my go-to memory when I'm gone."

"Thank you," he says, his teeth worrying my bottom lip. "I want you to know... when I touch you with my gift, I see beyond your quips and your deflections. I love the man who's still finding himself in here." He presses his hand to my heart and smiles up at me, his gaze content. "I love you, Bear."

I wrap my arms tighter around him. Tipping my head, I press my cheek against the top of his head and breathe in his earthy scent. "I love you too, Wolf. Soul deep."

~

*Calli*

The three of us hang back from the tunnel and give Kotah and Brant their moment. My talk with Margo may have given me new insight into Brant's motivations, but in the end, the thing he needs most is to learn to trust the four of us for the long-term. That won't happen overnight and that's okay.

He's worth the wait.

By the time the lust vibrating along the mating bond strengthens and then falls quiet, Hawk is catching up on FCO admin stuff on his laptop, and Jaxx and I are folding the freshly cleaned linens. "See, we can be good houseguests."

Jaxx chuckles. "Although it's far less entertaining than you throwing fireballs at Hawk and his ex and almost burning down the Fae Palace. I hope they didn't paint over the burn marks."

I chuckle and stack the towels on the dryer. "Riley would've loved to see that."

He nods. "How you doin' on that front? Have you been hearing her still?"

I shrug. "A few words in my head now and then, but nothing like the convo I had with her when I fainted at the palace. Maybe it's not real and I'm crazy or maybe it's my subconscious burping up what I need to hear when I need to hear it. I have no idea."

"Meh, whatevs. Who are we to judge, right? If hearin' her pearls of encouragement makes things a little easier in the worst moments, what does it matter what it is?"

I don't even bother trying to tame the fitted sheet, so I ball it up and plop it on top of the towels.

Jaxx chuckles and snatches it out of the basket, before doing a spectacular job of folding it straight and flat.

"Hello? Are you related to Martha Stewart or something? How'd you do that?"

"Mama taught me when I moved out on my own. She said no son of hers would be livin' like a college frat boy. I might be a bachelor, but one day knowin' how to keep a proper house would impress the right girl."

"Score one for Mama. Color me impressed."

"Mama's rarely wrong," he says. "And you didn't answer my question. Riley? How is your heart healin'?"

I inventory my emotions. "I'm still a work in progress. It will be five weeks tomorrow since I found her in that alley. In some ways, I can't believe it's been that long. In other ways, I'm incredibly thankful that I've had you four and the whole transitioning into a firebird to focus on. The past three weeks have flown by."

"Are we good to head out now?" Hawk asks, his bag slung over his shoulder. "Our ride should be here in the next few minutes and we still have to drive up to the main house and say our goodbyes."

"We're ready," Kotah says coming to get us. "Sorry for the holdup."

I wave that away and make a note of thanking Brant for putting that smile on Kotah's face. Whatever they shared washed away all the 'back to the palace' tension he'd been carrying since the plan was made. "Don't apologize, sugar. Nothing is more important than us getting ourselves sorted out. If that sounds selfish, I don't care. Fuck the world. If the foundation of our quint is flawed our love won't withstand the tornadoes."

Jaxx snorts. "Well, considering you're headed to Kansas to face the Fae Council and the Prime and Prima, I think it's a safe bet we'll be headed into a twister or two."

The helicopter ride to the private airstrip in Oregon takes less than an hour. Lukas arrives with Doc, Keyla, and her two security officers shortly after that. Hawk said their drive from the new rental property would take them twenty minutes, but he wasn't sure where they were staying because he had nothing to do with situating them. Unsure what was being tracked, he had Doc research and book the second property, so nothing tied back to him or his accounts.

Kotah bolts from the hangar the moment they arrive and hugs his sister. She looks as sad and emotional as her brother. It doesn't matter that they have shitty parents, death hurts.

"Hey, girlfriend," I say, once they come inside. "I'm so sorry about your father and all this falling on the two of you."

Keyla sighs. "We knew it was coming. It's been nice though, getting away for a bit." Her gaze travels across the hangar toward Doc and the smile that blooms tells me all I need to know. I tilt my head toward where he's standing with Hawk and Brant. "That good is he?"

Kotah follows my gaze and frowns. "What? You and Doc? When did that happen?"

Her blush is too cute. "It hasn't—yet. He says it's hands-off until he talks with you. Can you believe that? My brother gets a say in whether or not he'll fool around with me?"

"Well then, no," Kotah says matter-of-factly. "The answer is no."

I snort and wave that away. "You can summarily decide your sister's love life."

"Why not? If the question is mine to answer, why can't I keep my sister young and innocent forever."

Keyla laughs and leans close, drawing a deep breath. "You're a year older than me and wear the mark of your quint. If you get four lovers, why can't I have one?"

"I'm guessing, 'Because I said so,' won't work here?"

I laugh. "No. I don't think it will."

After Kotah pounding Brant in the face and the two of them declaring their love, I'm the last person who claims to understand what goes on in a man's head.

Still, I try to offer Keyla something to cheer her up. "If they both care about you, and I have no doubt about that, I'm sure it'll be fine. Right, Kotah?"

Kotah is still scowling at Doc across the room when he takes Keyla's hand. "I'll speak to him later. Right now, I want to know how you are. Was Mother decent to you?"

She nods. "Yeah. I think she's too panicked about Father to engage. You, on the other hand, she'll likely come at either with both barrels blazing or laying on the saccharine sweet support to try to win you over."

"Neither will work."

"No. And that's good. I didn't mention the micro-chipping on the phone. I figured we'd drop that bombshell together when you guys think it's most effective."

"Lukas mentioned you were chipped too. Are you all right? He said you wouldn't let him get rid of it."

She pulls a locket out from under her blouse and opens it up. Nestled inside are three tiny square slips of silver. "I didn't let him get rid of the others, either."

"Why is that?" I ask.

The locket clicks when she shuts it and she drops it back into her blouse. "Because with us heading back to the palace, it makes no sense. If Kotah and I are at the palace, people will know. If our tracking devices aren't registering there, we lose a tactical advantage. We should keep our discovery of them a secret for as long as we can. Then we can use it to our advantage in a crunch."

"I told you I saw great things in her," Hawk says smiling. He steps behind my hair and kisses the top of my head. "Well thought out, Keyla. Lukas studied them and figures they've got a range of about a mile, give or take, so yes, by all means, take them with you. Then we'll all be accounted for should somebody be looking for us."

"But you're not coming to the palace?" she asks.

"No, Brant, Lukas, and I are headed to California to catch up with my team tracking down the gifted kids."

Keyla frowns. "I wish we didn't have to split up all the time. I feel better when we're all in one place."

"Preach," I say, holding up my fist for a bump. "And how do I train at the palace without anyone realizing I can transform now and fly?"

"You can't," Hawk says.

"You *can?*" Keyla asks, lighting up. "When did that happen? You got air?"

"After I got kidnapped. Car explosion. Phoenix flight. Crash and burn. The decimation of a wheat field. I'll fill you in later. Hawk has to train me to land, but my take-off and flying are going good."

"And it's an absolute secret," Hawk says. "Nobody can know how close she is to being able to open the portal gate."

Keyla blinks. "Why do I feel like I've missed a lot?"

"Because you have," Kotah says. "But we'll catch you up on the flight."

Jaxx lets off a whistle across the hangar and waves for us all to gather. "Load up, people. The plane's ready to roll. Our destinies await."

# CHAPTER NINETEEN

Kotah

eyla, Doc, and her two security guards, FitzGibbons—Patrick Fitz and Mark Gibbons—board the plane and leave the five of us in the hangar green room, not wanting to say goodbye… again.

"No one walks the halls of the palace alone," Hawk says. "We don't know who we can trust so we trust only us, got it?"

Jaxx nods. "I'll take care of them. I promise."

Brant frowns. "Be safe, you guys."

I hug him. It's funny, he's got a full foot of height and more than a hundred pounds on me, but it feels like it's me crushing him. "You too, Bear. Find those kids and then we can put at least one part of this mess behind us."

He pulls back and his gaze falls to my lips. Indecision wars in his whiskey-colored eyes. Yeah, the others know what went on between us back in the tunnel of the bunker, but that was private. "May I?"

I meet his lips and he grips my braid at the nape of my neck. His tongue makes a lazy sweep into my mouth and tastes of chocolate. Ha!

I knew he snagged the last brownie. Expecting a quick goodbye, I'm surprised when he lingers.

When he pulls away, he swallows. "Thanks for loving me, Wolf. I'm bound to piss you all off more often than not, but I want this. I've wanted it from the first moment."

I kiss him again. "Come home soon."

While he moves to say goodbye to Calli, I shift to Hawk. I hug him without invitation and smile when he doesn't stiffen for the first time. My gift tingles over my skin and it's amazing how much more at peace he is now. "The matings agree with you."

He dips his chin. "I'm beginning to think you're right."

Now it's me who's awkwardly staring at Hawk's lips and I repeat Brant's question to me. "May I?"

Hawk's kiss is nothing like Brant's. Our avian is dominant and I submit to what he's willing to offer. It's short and then it's over. "Be careful, Wolf. Stick with Calli and Jaxx and let them watch your back. You're entering an enemy camp. Don't forget that."

"I won't."

Hawk's kiss with Jaxx is about the hottest thing I've ever seen. They each cup the jaw of the other and lock their lips with a force of passion I yearn to share one day. Watching them stirs my cock in my pants but I can't look away.

"This," Calli says, staring at the same display.

"This," I repeat, knowing exactly what she means.

"Keep that dance card close at hand, avian," Jaxx says, a throaty purr rolling from this throat. "We've got a date, for round two, yeah?"

Hawk's eyes flash with the wildness of his animal. "Yeah, we do. Looking forward to it."

"Okay, you two," Calli says, breathy. "You're killing us, over here. Either we gotta move or we gotta get naked."

Hawk chuckles and comes over to kiss her goodbye. "Be safe Spitfire. Try not to kill anyone until I get back to bury the bodies, 'kay?"

"No promises."

〜

*Calli*

We leave Hawk and Brant standing outside the hangar and wave while we taxi off in the Gulfstream. With heavy hearts we land five hours later in Kansas, get into the shuttle car, and make our way to the palace. "It's crazy, eh? How a few days can change the dynamic? I feel like we just tore half our heart out and left them behind."

"Same," Jaxx says.

"Same," Kotah agrees. "Although, that kiss you shared with Hawk might keep we warm for a few nights at least. Holy hell, Jaxx."

I bark a laugh. "Right?"

Jaxx snorts. "You two are hilarious."

I wave that away. "Ohmygod, Jaxx. Do you honestly not realize how smoking hot the chemistry is between you two?"

Jaxx chuckles and sits deeper in his seat. "You ain't seen nothing yet."

"Oh, but we want to… don't we Kotah?"

Kotah grins and rubs a palm across the fly of his pants. "More than anything. Now, however, might not be the time to be envisioning such things. I should at least attempt to keep up appearances as the son in mourning, shouldn't I?"

Jaxx laughs. "You mean the next Fae Prime shouldn't run around with an impressive party ragin' in his pants?"

"No. I think it would be considered poor taste."

Knowing that Kotah abhors the idea of facing a crowd head-on, I lean forward and speak to the driver. "Could you drop us off at the west entrance, please?"

The man's brow tightens as he meets my gaze in the rear-view mirror. "His Highness should be greeted at the main entrance, as is proper, milady. I was instructed to take you there by the Palace Liaison."

I look at Kotah and he frowns. "Raven. She must have her reasons."

"But you're the one with the crown, aren't you?"

He nods. "Good point. The west entrance if you will. I'd prefer to avoid the fanfare in my time of grief. My mates and I are tired and simply want to get inside and settle before we face what is to come."

"Yes, Majesty."

*Brant*

Our helicopter ride to Northern California is uneventful and Lukas, Hawk, and I take the time to go over what each of us knows about the continued search for the missing teens. Not one of the four who were recovered in Oregon were one of the kids I took into custody. I'm sure it's partly guilt for my part in their life's upheaval that has me obsessed, but the bigger part is being a kid with a wiped out past and knowing how bad it sucks not to know who you are or who your parents were.

"And you were able to speak with Hannah and confirm that she's alright?" I ask.

Lukas closes the file in his hands and passes it back to Hawk. "Yes. She's fine. The call to you was accidental but seeing as how it got everyone mobile and moving, we'll consider it divine intervention."

"Okay. As long as she's okay."

Hawk's brow arches. "If you care about this one and we're at a place to share advice, I'll warn you to tamp that down in front of Calli. After being on the receiving end of her wildling's flaming fury, I wouldn't wish her possessive rage on anyone I care about."

"Jayne escaped unharmed though, yeah?"

Hawk chuffs. "I said anyone I *care* about. I would've served Jayne up to get burned to a crisp if it wouldn't have hurt Calli more. Instead, it was poor Lukas here who bore the brunt of that battle."

He chuckles. "Living the adventure one day at a time."

I scratch my head. "I wish I hadn't been so out of it for that. Sounds like one helluva scene."

"Hawks right. It's nothing you want to revisit." Lukas gets up and heads up to the cockpit to check in with the pilot.

"More to love is more to lose," Hawk says, staring out the window at the clouds wisp past. "My nanny once said that to me, when I asked her why my dad didn't love me. I never really understood it until that moment when Calli went limp in my arms."

"You never risked love until her?"

He shakes his head, still staring off. "I never risked anything of myself until this mating. Funny, eh? People looking at me from the outside, thinking I had everything life could offer. There were times I would've agreed with them…"

"But not now?"

"No. Not now." He pulls his attention from his musings and smiles. "Sorry. I'm getting a little too introspective. Where were we?"

"We were building a list of people in your company who have the clout to pull something like this off."

"Right. Jayne Trenton, my PA, comes from old money and plenty of power. She has the run of the company. Hunter Gable, my Director of Operations, is a coyote shifter and always seems to have his fingers in everyone's assholes. I've got an eight-person executive team. They have influence but report to Jayne, so if there's collusion, they could be involved."

"Me," Lukas says, sliding back into his seat. "If you're making a comprehensive list, I should be included. I have all the clearances and respect within the company to get people to do what I ask without raising suspicion."

Hawk raises a brow. "I'm not concerned about you."

He shakes Hawk off. "Put me on the list. We don't want any blind spots."

I jot him down but agree with Hawk that it's a waste of ink. "Who takes over if a non-confidence gets leveled against you by the Fae Council?"

"No one. It's my company. No board of directors to answer to. The company lives or dies by my hand."

"Okay, then who succeeds you if you drop dead from a heart attack or you know… get shot twice and bleed out?"

Hawk waggles his brow at that. "Hopefully that was a one-time deal. Thank you, by the way. Jaxx told me you took on some nasty guard dogs and kept me from getting chewed."

I shrug. "Score it as a point in the win column for me for later. I'm sure I'll do something to piss you off soon enough."

"I'm sure," Hawk says, chuckling. "Up until the mating, my successor would've been Byron Maass. He's been with my company for almost two decades and helped me put together the Fae Council. He knows all the players and how the FCO works."

"Until the mating? That changed?"

He nods. "Of course. In the event of my untimely demise, everything transfers to my four mates equally. Did I forget to mention that, Bear? You're a multi-millionaire."

I blink as that sinks in. Even with all the bad blood, he thought of me that way? Yeah, I truly am a tunnel-visioned meathead. "Well, hot dayam. I guess I can afford the new transmission for my old truck after all."

Hawk chuckles. "I guess you can."

~

*Jaxx*

"Welcome back to the Timber Trail suite," Kotah says as we let ourselves into the same door we were kicked out of not that long ago. "Home sweet home."

Calli and I look at each other and snort. "Not!"

Although, once we step inside, I wonder about that. "What the hell happened in here?"

Gone are the bedroom doors on either end of the suite with a living room in the middle. The place has been gutted and completely remodeled, including opening the ceiling so it's now a two-story space with exposed wooden beams, a beautiful staircase, and a wood and glass railing above. The entire space bursts with the warmth of honeyed-pine construction, slate floors, ruby and gold accents, and welcoming energy.

Kotah smiles. "Do you like it? I was very specific about what I wanted. I'm supposed to take the royal suite, but I hate it there. This is the only place in the palace other than the kitchen courtyard and gazebo that means anything to me. And I couldn't let them paint over that."

He points to the wall behind the door and I let off a whoop. "You saved Calli's fireball wall. That's awesome."

"Somewhere between that and when you passed out and flashed your junk to my mother was when I fell in love with all of you. I didn't want to lose those memories or leave them to anyone else."

"So, you brought Northwood Hall to Kansas," Calli says, grinning from ear to ear. "I love it."

Kotah exhales. "I'm so relieved you're happy. You gave me the idea."

"I did," Calli says, kicking off her sneakers. "Yay, me."

Kotah drops his and Calli's bags onto the leather sectional and takes her hand to guide her up the stairs. They walk halfway across, to the edge of the railing over by the second door, and then face me down on the main floor.

"Do you remember what you said when we were standing right here when I first gave you the tour of Northwood Hall?" He wraps her in a playful embrace from behind, cupping her breasts and kissing the back of her neck.

She lets off a nervous laugh. "I remember your cock being solid against my ass and you grinding me like you are now. Then you said you needed me naked and wanted inside me to christen the place as mates."

He laughs. "All true. Then I told you that was where I felt the most myself. In that space. And you said…"

I laugh down below at Calli's face. She's definitely pulling a blank. "I think you lost her at want inside you. She gets distracted."

Calli giggles and lifts her top to flash me her tits. "True story. Sorry, sugar. What did I say?"

"You said, 'Whatever you need, sweet wolf.' And that gave me the idea. I need that moment, that feeling of being at home with my mates. If I could have that here, I might be able to breathe."

"Well, you've got my vote," I say, jogging up with the bags to settle in. "Are the rooms laid out in the same floorplan as Northwood?"

Kotah nods. "Mostly, though I made our master bedroom bigger and put in a door to access the bedroom next door so Hawk doesn't feel separated from us. I also made us a full office suite for Hawk and me to work in regularly and an extra desk for you guys if something comes up. Downstairs, I converted the two bedrooms on that end of the suite into a workout and fitness room so we don't have to move the couch every time we want to train, and the two bedrooms on that end are a man cave and a library."

Calli's smile lights up. "You did good, Wolf."

He bites his lower lip. "*Annnnd,* I may have added a few perks to the spare room too. I had Hawk help me order what we need to furnish our adult playroom."

"Hot, damn," I say, my interest in the remodel suddenly getting much more focused. "Which one?" When Kotah points, I pick up speed. I jog past the two of them and yep… worth the price of admission. "Yessss, look at this."

"Holy shit," Calli says her eyes widening to round saucers. "You went full-on kinky minx on us, Kotah. I don't know what half this stuff is."

"Me either," he says, grinning. "But it'll be fun to find out. Don't you agree?"

I give him a high-five and my jaguar lets off a languid, long purr. I'm looking at the leather cuffs and the bondage restraints and the blindfolds and I swear my mouth starts to water. "Hells to the yeah. We're trying out this sex swing tonight, but first…"

I close the door and push the ideas lighting off in my head down for the time being, "we've got business to take care of. And when I say business, I mean food and figuring out who's trying to screw us over and why."

# CHAPTER TWENTY

Hawk

*W*e land on the private property of one of the Pacific Coast ursine communities north of a mountain town called Willow Creek. It's a heavily forested area of seclusion, remote access roads, and low populations. It the perfect place for a community of bear wildlings to live undetected by the human world and maybe fae conspirators trying to stay off our radar.

"We've got a vehicle here for you," the Six Rivers Alpha says when he greets us. "And Ben called down and explained what you're facing. I've got my sleuth and the Redwood sleuth on notice in case you need backup."

"Thank you, Alpha," Brant says.

He smiles at Brant and shakes his head. "I always pictured you mating one of my girls, Robbins. But, I suppose there's no arguing with the Guardians of the Phoenix prophecy, is there?"

"No sir. And I would've been a lucky man to have any of your girls as my mate. They are treasures, every one of them."

He seems pleased with the bear's praise. "And you think it'll happen? You believe your phoenix will be able to break the portal block between the two realms?"

"Calli has a way to go in claiming her powers," I say, reminding Brant that we need to protect her progress.

Brant nods. "She transitioned less than a month ago. It'll take her some time, but she'll do it. I have no doubt."

Lukas starts up the truck and we extend our thanks. In another few minutes, we stop at the end of the lane, and Lukas programs our destination on the nav system. "Team two is sitting on a heavily treed property twenty minutes north of here. I texted them that we're on our way and asked for someone to call with a sit-rep."

Lukas's phone rings and the vehicle's Bluetooth flips it onto the console. "You're on speaker with me, Mr. Barron, and Brant Robbins. What have you got, Griggs?"

"Uh… honestly, we aren't sure," Griggs says. "An eight-foot-tall creature shrouded in shadow portaled onto the grounds an hour ago in the company of three teens. They went inside, but whether they're still in there is anyone's guess."

"Tell me about the creature," I say.

"None of us has seen anything like it."

"Describe it to me."

"Tall, like I said… with a massive rack of antlers rising from the back of his head. The horns spread and speared the width of his broad shoulders and then some. He walked on two legs, but his arms were elongated and looked like he could drop to all four and become a beast in battle if needed."

"Did he wear the curled horn of a ram around his neck?"

"Yeah. We wondered about that. You know it?"

"Yeah. I know it," I say, cold dread twisting in my guts. "That is a greater fae known as a Forest Lord. And that horn is used to call his dire hounds. Stay the hell back and if he sees you, do *not* engage. On second thought if you're discovered and he advances, run like hell."

I cast a glance at the driver's seat and Lukas nods. "Going much faster."

"I take it that Forest Lords are big baddies?" Brant says in the back.

I chuff. "You mean mythical beings of untold power and fury that control a pack of satanic hounds that rip people to shreds… yeah, that would be them."

"Awesome." He leans forward between the seats. "Were the three teens with Antler Man from your site or from another site and brought there?"

"What are you thinking," I ask.

"Maybe they realized Oregon was breached. They could be consolidating to keep a closer eye on their captives."

"I couldn't say," Griggs says.

"Very well," I say, staring at my clenched fists in my lap. "We'll be there shortly. Do nothing until we arrive." When the line goes dead and the radio comes back online, I let off a string of curses. "We don't have the power to take on a Forest Lord."

"Nope." Lukas hits the indicator and makes a left.

"Can you phone a friend?"

The side of his mouth lifts in a mocking smile. "You mean can I call the Mage's Guild and ask for volunteers to infiltrate a blind situation and take on a Forest Lord we know nothing about and the wrath of his evil hounds?"

"Yeah."

"No."

I scrub a hand through my hair. "Who the fuck is behind this teen kidnapping that a Forest Lord is involved?"

"Maybe *he* is," Brant says, his voice more growl than usual. "Maybe he's our Black Knight."

I wave that off. "Creatures of their age and power don't care about modern politics and control. They value old ties and the ways of the past. If someone told me there was one involved in this mess, I would've bet money he'd be on *our* side, helping us open the gate for the chance of reuniting with others of his kind still in StoneHaven."

"Assuming there are any left in StoneHaven," Lukas says. "Weren't they one of the first targets when the power struggles began?"

"Maybe that's why he's on this side," Brant says. "He saw the writing on the wall for his extermination way back when and defected to stay alive."

I press my fingers over the throb taking root behind my left eye. "Well, if he intended to remain unknown and stay alive, I'd say he succeeded. I had no clue a greater fae of his level lived on this side of the gate."

"Awesome," Brant says. "I love me some insurmountable odds. Maybe we'll get extra lucky and they also have swarms of hellwasps or a phane under their control. Let's make things interesting."

I meet Lukas's gaze and sigh. "Ignore the babble in the back seat. He gets smart-mouthy when the world crashes in."

"Fuck you, Hawk."

"Already offered. I declined. Take the hint."

The low chuckle in the back isn't what I expect, but it's better than losing our minds considering the situation. "I'm glad you're into kink. I'm already visualizing the duct tape over your mouth."

Okay, that was decent. "Remember, it's mind over matter, Bear. I don't mind because you don't matter."

"The word of the day is 'closure,' avian. Try to keep your thoughts out of my pants. My zipper is closed for business."

"Fine, Bear, I'll be your sex object. Whenever you bring up sex, I'll object."

"It's true, I've been missing you lately, but my aim is getting better."

I laugh. "I'm trying to see things from your point of view, but I'm not sure I'll ever get my head stuck that far up my ass."

"Sorry, Hawk. I couldn't fail to agree with you less than I already don't."

Lukas sends me a look and shakes his head. "If you two are finished, we're here."

I sober and shrug. "If we don't laugh and let off steam we're going to explode."

He turns and pulls the keys, and the engine falls quiet. "I'm used to you choosing the explode option. You laughing freaks me out."

∼

*Calli*

Jaxx and I putter around the suite while Kotah and Keyla visit their father. Doc is with them, so he'll watch their backs. In the meantime, Jaxx and I start redecorating the cork wall of the office pinning up printouts of who the likely suspects are in this conspiracy. Brant sent us their list and we were adding to it, trying to make some desperately needed connections. After an hour, we're looking at almost thirty faces and no idea how any of it fits together.

"So, we have the council here, the palace people here, and the FCO corporate people here," Jaxx says. "Now we start looking into connections we didn't consider."

"Like what?" I ask, pointing to the last slice of pizza.

"You eat it," Jaxx says. "Like, say… does Raven belong to a Darkside support group? Or does Jayne get down and dirty with Dane from the Fae Council? I don't know. Do I look like Sherlock Holmes?"

I chuckle. "Thankfully, no."

There's a knock at the door and we jog downstairs to receive our first visitor. In the hall, I find a lady-sized raccoon holding a two-level pie keeper. The top is coconut cream and the middle looks like a raspberry flan. Both are favorites of Kotah's I'm assuming.

"Adahy, come in." She accepts the invitation and joins us in the suite. She's dressed in a silk blouse topped by a suede vest and green leather pants similar to those she had on the day I first met her.

Jaxx doesn't miss a beat and offers his hand. "Kotah's weapon's master and confidante, correct? He speaks of you kindly. Welcome."

"A housewarming gift for my boy and his mates," she says, handing Jaxx the pie keeper. "I went to the royal suites first, but Raven sent me here and said my boy is not residing in the Prime wing."

"No," Jaxx says, sliding the pies into the fridge for later. "Keyla and her mother will be free to stay there, but Kotah thought this suite would be more to his liking."

She looks around, her bushy ringed tail swishing in the air behind her. "I agree. He always was happiest at Northwood Hall. Good for him."

"It's perfect, isn't it?" I say.

"It is. Now, just to be clear. I am moving to the suite across the hall later today. From now on, I am the only one to cook for you and your guests. I will be the only one to present food and drink to you unless you cook for yourself. And if you do cook for yourself, I will stock your kitchen supplies myself, understood?"

I nod, feeling the weight of her words. "Has something happened?"

"Not yet," she says, preening her whiskers with black, leathery fingers, "but I know that conniving bitch and I'll not let her drug my boy into an obedience stupor as she has his father for all these years."

"The Prime has been drugged?"

She nods. "I'd bet my butt it's why he's dying so young. Not natural that."

"And you think Kotah will be next?" Jaxx asks, looking as horrified as I feel.

"She'll try, don't doubt it for a moment. When I caught her doing it to the Prime, she had me discredited and days later I was cursed into this form. A freak accident they said. No. It was her… I've always known it. She may have removed me from preparing the royal meals back then and fooled everyone since, but the table is about to turn."

I'm not sure what my expression looks like but Adahy nods. "And while you are here, I will instruct you on weapon combat. I may not be the warrior woman I once was, but short arms don't erase a century of master weaponry. Show me where you will train. I will ensure you have what we need."

Jaxx looks as shellshocked as I feel. "It's over here."

Adahy takes a tour of the workout room and pulls a tablet out of the side pocket in her green, leather pants. "I'll make a list. It won't take me long. My boy can approve it when he gets back and we'll get started tomorrow."

I nod, feeling like I'm caught in the whirlwind that is Adahy. "Does Kotah know about his mother?"

"What about her?" Adahy asks, focused on the tablet.

"About her drugging the Fae Prime. Does he know?"

Adahy blinks up at me and frowns. "No. The Prima isn't the one.

It's Raven. That bitch has this whole palace fooled. And yes, I told everyone with ears but no one believed me."

"Kotah never mentioned any of this."

She waves that away and continues to make her notes. "Prima said it was nonsense and Raven threatened to harm them if I continued to interfere. I couldn't put them in any more danger than they were already in. The Prima wouldn't listen. That woman is just as bad as... Oh, yes, I see your confusion. She is also a conniving bitch."

"So, Raven is the one we're looking out for?"

"Her and anyone working under her orders... which in this palace is *everyone*."

I look at Jaxx as something clicks. "Maybe it wasn't the Prima who had us attacked in Oregon. Raven was there and she could have ordered me kidnapped."

"She would've known to grab Keyla and draw Kotah away as your defender."

"And she was the only one of us not outside. She stayed in the house during the entire attack. If she knew what was happening and didn't want to get caught in the crossfire her hiding in the house makes sense."

Jaxx runs his fingers through his beautiful blond hair and whistles long and low. "I did not see that coming. Watson, I think we have our first suspect to investigate."

*Brant*

Hannah meets us out by the road and despite being told she was fine, it makes me feel better to see her for myself. It's not the same kind of relief I felt when I saw Calli wrapped in the fire blanket waiting for me outside Grant's fire station, but yeah, I definitely care.

"You scared the shit out of me, Hannah," I say, stopping myself before I hug her. "Where were you when you called and who was whimpering in the background?"

I was edging toward the cabin back here and our perps brought out one of the teens to bury. They had another one of the kids with the power to move earth, lift the soil for the shallow grave. That was the one crying you heard."

I growl. "They're killing them?"

She shakes her head. "I don't think it was intentional. From what we learned speaking to the four we rescued in Oregon, their captors were amping them up and then draining their power. It's hard on them. We'll know more when we exhume the body when this is over but we figure the one that died just couldn't withstand their process."

"This ends now," I say, swinging my gaze to Hawk.

"Agreed. Let's take these fuckers down."

Our group half slides, half runs down the backside of a rise, and then jumps a creek when we get to the bottom. Once across the water, I rip a strip off my shirt and tie the fabric to an oak sapling.

When Hawk arches a brow, I smile. "Lukas may not have phoned a friend, but I did. Along the Pacific Coast, we've got the right to bear arms and the right to arm bears. This is ursine territory, and bears don't take it well when bad guys fuck with our mojo."

"That Forest Lord will do more than fuck with your mojo, Bear. If he's here as an offensive force, blood will be spilled. Anyone here on your behalf is a life you're risking."

I grit my teeth and lift my chin. "Understood. We might seem like we're all brawn and little brain, but I promise you, the bears know the score. We know what's at stake here."

We follow Hannah back to where two other FCO officers are tucked behind natural blinds.

"Where are the other two?" Hawk asks. IO teams ride in groups of five.

Griggs stands from his position and Hannah relieves him to keep watch. "Hannaford circled to the west and Watkins treed himself to the east of the compound so he could get a look at what we're dealing with his long-range scope."

"What *are* we dealing with?" Hawk asks.

"From what we gather, Robbins hit the nail on the head when he wondered about them consolidating the teens. Those three teens that arrived were ushered upstairs into an open loft. Watkins counts eight in total."

"That's still one short on the tally," I say. "Even with one dead and buried, our lucky number is nine."

"I'm sorry to say Hannaford found another grave on the west end of the clearing. We're focusing on eight hostages inside that building."

*Two dead. Dammit.*

My bear roils inside me and pulls at my tether of control. The growl that rumbles free of my chest is nothing I can control or contain. "I want to fucking rip these people in two."

Hawk sets his hand against my neck and looks at me straight on. His touch does more than any casual contact should. With the five of us mated to Calli, and Kotah and Jaxx, and Jaxx and Hawk mated as well, our bond grows stronger by the day.

He senses it too. The moment our connection fires, his gaze softens and his posture relaxes a little. "I know how you feel, Bear. First, we rescue the eight. Then you and your bear friends can make ribbons of anyone in there that's involved."

"Yeah? You're giving us free rein?"

He nods. "First we focus on the kids we can save."

"Agreed." I check my phone and check on the status of our backup. "The Cavalry is here. Giddy up."

# CHAPTER TWENTY-ONE

Kotah

"You're back." Calli greets me at the door of our suite with a soul-warming hug. The moment her forehead nuzzles into my neck, the power of our mate touch takes hold and the strain of visiting with my parents eases.

Jaxx joins in and wraps us both in his arms, pressing his lips to my throbbing temple. "Other than the obvious state of affairs, how'd it go?"

"There were no battles but enough looks and frowns to let me know that neither of them thinks there's any hope for the fae realm in my care."

"I'm sorry, sugar," Calli says. "But you know what? Fuck 'em if they can't take a joke. They forced you into the position. They can't then gripe that it's you that's there."

"That's what I told him," Keyla says. She and Doc shuffle past where we're blocking the doorway. "Holy crap, look at this place. It's exactly how we planned it."

Jaxx brushes his thumb over my cheek and then eases back. "You had a hand in the remodel too, did you?"

"Most of it," I say, drawing a deep breath and taking Calli's hand. "Though the furnishings Hawk and I purchased, I took care of myself."

The smile that warms Jaxx's face drains the rest of my stress away.

Calli releases my hand and moves to the refrigerator. "Adahy stopped by and left us a housewarming gift. You up for some pie?"

"We have cookies too," Keyla says, holding up a covered plate. She pulls one out and takes a big bite. "Chocolate nut. Raven gave them to us on our way out."

Jaxx launches forward and smacks the cookie from her hand and my mouth drops open.

"What the hell, Jaxx?" Keyla snaps.

Calli takes the plate from Keyla and covers them back up. "Does the palace have a science lab?"

"On lower-level two," I say. "Why do you ask? What's gotten into you two?"

Jaxx fills us in on Adahy's visit and I'm shocked.

"I don't believe it," Keyla says, looking even more skeptical than I'm sure I do. Then again, she's never been as close with Adahy as I am and is closer with Raven. During the past couple of years, while I was away at university, they grew to be friends. "No one is controlling Father. He's simply a cold, closed-minded male."

"One way to find out," Calli says, handing the cookies to Doc. "Take these to the lab and oversee the testing. You know the most about drugs and chemicals of all of us. Don't let the tech make any calls or leave the room. I don't want it to get out what we're doing."

Doc nods. "I'll handle it. Maybe Kotah can call down and give the royal okay, so they don't question it."

"No need," Keyla says. "I'm going too. I'll show you where the labs are and then we'll prove Raven's not involved in anything duplicitous."

I take her hand and nod. "I honestly hope you're right, but remember what Hawk said. We can only trust us until we know who's moving behind the scenes against us."

It's clear Keyla disagrees, but she squeezes my hand and nods her understanding. "Miss me while I'm gone."

I chuckle. "I always do."

*Brant*

The thing I've always loved most about being a FCO Enforcer was knowing I was heading into a fight and feeling the surge of adrenaline kick in. I've never been arrogant enough to think myself invincible. But I am cocky enough to know I've got better than average odds. Standing behind a screen of trees in the wooded hillside of my wildling territory, nothing fits quite right. I breathe in the loamy moisture of the forest. I see and feel my bear brethren shifting and ambling all around me.

Tonight, the thrill doesn't take hold.

I don't want to be here.

At some time during the past three weeks, my priorities shifted. As much as I want to fight the good fight and free these kids. I can't help thinking I'm not where I should be.

Calli, Kotah, and Jaxx are halfway across the country in a den of vipers and my heart and focus are with them. Wondering about them. Worrying about them.

"Head on a swivel, Bear," Hawk says. "Don't you get dead on me."

I grip the shoulder straps of his Kevlar flack vest and try to anchor myself. "You almost bit it on our last field trip. I don't want to go through that again."

Hawk looks like he's about to say something flippant but stops himself. He leans forward and touches his forehead to mine. "We stick together, mate. You and me. No matter what else happens around us, we're joined at the hip. I promised Calli we'd both come back to her in one piece. Don't make a liar out of me."

I nod and shift to my bear form.

The woods quietly heave with furred bodies weaving through the trees around us. In my wildling form, I stand chest level with my mate. He walks beside me, one hand on my shoulder, and scrubs his fingers through my thick, grizzly fur. "You know, Bear, you're a hell of a lot more badass than I give you credit for."

*Now he tells me?* I lift my snout to him and let off a grunt.

"What's that? You think I'm even more incredible than you? Thanks, Bear. It's good of you to finally recognize it."

*Asshole.* I grunt again.

He ruffles the side of my furry head and laughs. "All right. Let's do this."

With the whistle of a bird call, he signals for everyone to start our approach. Griggs, Hannaford, and Watkins are leading an advanced team focused on the extraction of the teens.

We are in charge of the offense and bad guys.

At least, that's how it's supposed to go.

"We've got movement in the house," Hawk whispers, tapping the comm earpiece and waiting until I nod.

My bear brothers drift in and out of the trees around us. We blend well into the natural landscape and our scents fill the night air. Full-dark has fallen and masks our approach. Hannah and Lukas swept the area for warding spells and perimeter alarms. Everything is a go.

I keep my senses on high-alert—hearing, sight, smell...

The breeze changes course and a host of new scents hit the receptors in my nose. They aren't wildling scents, and they aren't natural woods scents... they're fae. Definitely fae.

Bodies rustle in the underbrush. The movement is faint. I prick my ears and freeze.

Hawk tenses beside me and draws his gun.

"Ambush!"

The woods explode to life as cast-magic lights up the sky above the trees. Lunging into formation, we charge the attacking foes. The trees are a harried mess of clashing bodies.

A brown bear I know tackles a female with purple hair and glowing hands. Lukas takes on two hyenas fighting in tandem.

I let a roar tear from my throat and stand on my back paws. Hawk gives me an appreciative glance and then signals for me to follow him as he cuts through the opposing forces.

After three gallops, I pass him and start mowing over our opponents. He finds he's more effective in his human form, but I worry about him. Neither human nor hawk is as strong and menacing as he needs to be in situations like this.

The attacking force seems surprised to be facing such strong opposition. Maybe they only knew about team two acting as our scouting party. Maybe they thought they'd be picking off easy targets. Sucks to be them.

I can make out traces of different races as we break through the trees and reach the two-story ranch-style cabin where the teens are being held.

By the long, pointed ears and straggly blond hair, we've got drow, the guy with the grotesquely long arms and rippling muscles is a rugaru, then we've got the beaked faces of an orc, the green-tinged ugliness of a goblin, and the boxy, no-neck, barrel-body of trolls.

None of that registers as much of a threat.

What has me peeing a little is the eight-foot caribou man standing on the front lawn with his eyes glowing silver.

Hawk raises the sight of his gun and braces his arms. He jogs out, arms poised. "Why are you here, Forest Lord? Are you bound to these men? Are they bound to you?"

Cue the cackle of evil laughter.

I cringe. "What business is it of yours?"

"What business is this of yours? We two are Guardians of the Phoenix. These men are involved in a plot to stop us from opening the portal gate. I would think you'd want to reunite with your kind."

"You know neither my mind nor my heart's desire, wildling. If you did, you wouldn't be so calm." He lifts the horn hanging around his neck and presses it to his lips.

Hawk unloads his gun, first shooting the Forest Lord and then ricocheting bullets off his enchanted dog whistle. The bullets hit their target but bounce off without effect.

The echo of something unholy rends the air and I feel more than hear the rabid snarls of the dire hounds as they are drawn from the annals of hell. Shadows pull from the ground and form demon dogs that take physical form. They flank their master, their eyes glowing red, their fangs dripping with frothy saliva.

For a moment time freezes and my mind spins into fast forward. My heart quits beating and stalls out in my chest. Hawk is too close. If those hounds launch into an attack, I'll never get in front of him fast enough to shield him.

Panic spikes through my veins and Hawk's comment from the plane rings in my head. "More to love is more to lose."

Except, I won't entertain the idea of losing Hawk. Jaxx is right. The five of us are becoming a family. Five. Of. Us. Hawk can't be taken down by a giant antler freak. I can't allow that.

I suck in a breath and the world flips back into real-time.

I call on the strength in my muscles, the strength of my will, and the strength in my belief that the five of us have more destiny in front of us.

My roar shakes the trees around me and I launch forward.

I don't go for Hawk or the hounds, I go for the source of power. I bolt straight at the Forest Lord himself. Several of my ursine kin see my plan and join the attack.

In one of those slow-motion moments in life, both sides assessed the other. I see the Forest Lord for the ultimate power he is and he sees that I don't expect to win this battle... but I will do enough damage that the bears who come after me will finish my fight.

The freak's crooked sneer slips from his face as I sweep his leg and take him to the ground. The hounds attack and the daggers of their fangs rip through my thick pelt.

The sharp bang of Hawk's gun going off does nothing to slow the attack. The hounds are made of shadows and vapor. Bullets won't get them off my back.

Fae roar in the woods all around us.

Foul magic, wild and tainted with dark energy sears my body like a swarm of hellwasps stinging me all at once. I curse myself for manifesting that idea.

Hawk yells something and a glowing sword appears in his hand.

He's got Lukas's magic in his blood from the transfusion and he uses it to swipe at the shadow beasts tearing at me.

The Forest Lord bellows beneath me and I almost lose my hold. Another bear's jaw closes on the antler man's wrist. He writhes, impaling my kin on his sharp, ivory horns. The tine breaks off in the bear's throat and his body convulses until it falls still. I roar as my vision fades.

I'm not afraid of dying but I cannot stand the thought of another dying in my place. For a moment, my sight fails me and I'm all sensation and instinct. The snap of bone and a burst of blood in my mouth gives me strength.

*You might not die, motherfucker, but you won't kill what's mine either.*

*I wanted none of this Guardian. This is not my choice.* The Forest Lord's words invade my cranium a split-second before he vanishes from beneath me. The magic from his portal tingles in my nose and I gag.

The sudden loss of tension beneath me makes me stumble off balance. My body sags, blood gushing from the wounds on my back and shoulders. The dire hounds are gone... their summoning lost when the Forest Lord fled.

A booming battle cry roars through the clearing, and the sounds of violence are replaced by heaving breath, pained growls, and baleful howls.

"Brant, shitshitshit." Hawk is there, grabbing at me with bloody hands. "Lukas! I need you. Don't you die on me, Bear."

*Die? Am I dying?*

"He needs a healing sleep," one of my kin says.

*Fuck that. I need to stay sharp and find out about the teens.*

"Hibernate, Bear," Hawk says, looking ill. "Sink into a healing sleep."

I strain my neck and let off a grunt.

Lukas rushes in from behind me and curses. He drops on the grass beside me and starts spouting off shit about bleeding out. *Um, hello . . . sitting right here.*

More cursing.

Hawk frowns and grips my cheeks with both hands, making eye-contact. His eyes are glowing with the full ascension of his alpha. "As your alpha mate, I command you to hibernate. Sink into full, healing sleep."

I don't get the option to argue. My bear recognizes Hawk's power and there's no fighting biology.

I close my eyes and give up my struggles.

# CHAPTER TWENTY-TWO

## Hawk

*a* knock at the stateroom door brings Lukas into the room with a tray of food. I sit up on the birthed mattress and scrub my hands over my face. "What time is it?"

"One o'clock."

I frown, my mind weighted under a wet, wool blanket of fog. "In the morning or afternoon?"

"Afternoon. We'll be landing soon. Eat and have a shower. I'll sit with him."

"I need to piss but other than that, I'll stay. He's better when I'm touching him. It's a bonding thing. It comforts him… all of us, actually."

Lukas offers me a sad smile. "He'll pull through. He's too stubborn not to."

I nod and roll toward the small lavatory at the back of my plane. The moment I stand, gravity makes things more urgent, and I hustle to get to where I'm going. "How are the teens?"

"Happy to be reunited. The twelve of them will spend the next few days in the care and protection of the bears and Griggs's team. Then, once you've spoken to Fiske, we'll make the arrangements to reinsert them into their lives with protected identities."

"Once we get Brant to the palace, I'd like you to fly back and go through the debriefing with them personally. I'd prefer to do it myself, but I can't." I shake off, get things put away, and wash up.

"I'll take care of it."

I collapse more than climb back onto the mattress. "Thank you, Lukas," I say, studying the dark circles under his eyes. "I know I ask too much of you."

He waves that off. "I'm more than your right-hand man, Barron. I'm your friend. And I'm also a concerned member of the fae community who wants to see things work out. If we have to double or triple the workload until Calli gets the gate open, that's what we'll do... but it'll happen."

I prop myself up against the wall of the plane and shift until my legs until they bump up against the rounded spine of my bear. He's been out cold since I commanded him to rest. It took over an hour and six bears taking turns lifting him, to get him out of the woods and back to the trucks, but his kin never complained and never let up. "You'll feel better, soon, Bear. I promise. Calli will take care of everything."

I hate to keep falling back on Calli healing us back from the brink, but she is—by far—Brant's best chance of survival.

I know I should call her and give her a head's up, but she'll go stir crazy and there's nothing to be done until we get there. When we're preparing for landing, I'll make the call to Jaxx and let them know we're coming.

Why have all of us sick with worry?

I set the tray over my lap and try not to think about the worst-case scenarios tripping around in my head. He'll be fine. I have to believe that.

"Barron, eat. You're no good to anyone if you don't take care of yourself."

I make a concerted effort to focus on the truth of that. There are two sandwiches on the tray, one of them is turkey with cranberry and brie, and the other is a roast beef dip with caramelized onions and provolone. My stomach lets off a wild roar of appreciation and I dig in.

"How are you so sure we'll get the gate open?"

He chuckles. "I've been at your side long enough to know that when you're set on a course, nothing stops you. With the others in the mix, I have no doubt."

I open the can of Coke and take a sip. "What do you think waits for us on the other side?"

He leans against the frame of the doorway and sighs. "Well, the prophecy was set not to trigger a phoenix until it was time to reunite the realms. I guess StoneHaven survived the civil wars and stabilized."

"That's hopeful."

"Maybe. You know me, sunshine and strawberries."

I snort and finish the turkey sandwich and start on the beef. "The two teens that died. I want their bodies exhumed and prepared in the traditions of their species, whatever they are. They'll get a proper send-off."

"Do you want their families unlocked too?"

I swallow past the lump in my throat. "It seems cruel to give people back the memories of children to simply tell them they were murdered."

"Agreed."

I dip the roast beef in the au juice and chew. "We'll honor them. We'll ensure they aren't forgotten."

"Prepare for landing," the captain says over the speaker.

I hand Lukas the tray and pull out my phone. "If you'll excuse me, I'll need a few minutes."

*Brant*

"Come on, Bear. Wake up."

I register the alpha timbre vibrating in my cells and follow Hawk's voice along the mating bond. Someone is stroking my ears and it feels so good. My bear lets off a rumble and I fight the pull of slumber. When I finally force my eyes open, I'm groggy and starving and confused about my surroundings.

The last thing I remember is taking on the Forest Lord and being attacked by his hounds. "You forced me to hibernate."

Hawk smiles, his hand still on the side of my face from scratching my ears. "And look at that. Despite popular belief, you can listen and do what you're told."

I blink and take in my mates all in the bed around me. "Tell me I didn't miss our first five-way. If there's going to be a mating orgy a man should at least be conscious."

Calli tightens her hold where she's draped over my chest. When she looks up, her eyes are red-rimmed and swollen. Score another one to the healing magic of our mate. "We'd never start without you, Bear. Who'd provide the sexy quips."

Jaxx clasps my hand and kisses my knuckles. "Glad to see your face, Bear."

"Glad to be seen."

Kotah is locked in against my left side and props himself up on his elbow. "We love you."

"I love you guys too," I say a bit overwhelmed. "Was it that close? I didn't think I was that bad off."

Hawk chuffs. "You took on a Forest Lord and his hounds. Yeah, it was that close. It was also reckless, unbelievably heroic, and slightly offensive because you did it to keep me from being attacked. We were supposed to be a team, Bear. You've got to trust us to take care of ourselves in a battle or you're going to get yourself killed."

"Case in point," Jaxx says pointing at me lying here.

"I'll work on it," I say. "I tend to be a little overprotective."

Calli wriggles on top of me and three sources of major discomfort become very immediate. I groan and ease her off to the side. "Are you okay, Bear?"

"Fine, beautiful," I say, kicking my leg over her and rolling off the bed. "Just naked and starving and have to piss like a racehorse. Your nearness to my cock wasn't doing me any favors on any front."

I head straight into the ensuite and close the door all but a crack. "Why are we at Northwood Hall? What did I miss?"

"We're not," Jaxx says. "We're at the palace. Kotah gave our Timber Trail suite a makeover."

"Nice. A home away from home."

"That's the idea," Kotah says.

I wash up, flash some clothes on, and when I go back out and see the worried glances, I rub the warm spot in my chest. "I'm good, guys. Better than good. Things are finally settling into place for me. I realized something in those woods."

Hawk looks up. "Oh? Something more than stay away from the pointy end of the Antler Man?"

"Yeah, more than that." I meet the caring gazes of my mates and pause to soak it in. "I didn't belong there. I wanted to be here, with you guys. All of you. That's not lip service, avian," I say, making sure he sees my sincerity. "I want you to believe me—to know that I'm all in."

Hawk dips his chin and meets me for a hug. "I'm glad to hear it, but you sorta already told me."

"I did?"

He eases back and pulls something from his pocket. "After the Forest Lord portaled out and you fell to the ground, you had this clenched in your hand."

My chest warms as the mating crystal in his hand starts to glow. Jaxx's and Kotah's must resonate at the same frequency because theirs start to glow too.

The pie-shaped gemstone rises from the palm of Hawk's hand and hovers between us, catching the sunlight from the window and casting prisms of greens and browns in every direction. Jaxx's crystal swirls like water, Kotah's is the essence of spirit, and mine is earth.

I raise my palm to accept it, my throat growing thick with emotion. "This is real, isn't it?"

"It's real," Jaxx says, bringing Calli and Kotah around Hawk to watch.

"Not the crystal... but us, this..." I say, blinking against the sting in my eyes as I gesture between the five of us.

"We're real," Calli says. "It's time you trust in a future with people who love you."

"We are the only true thing in my life," Kotah says, his voice filled with the unending serenity that is our wolf prince. "And this is only the beginning. I feel it to the full depth of my soul. There is greatness to come and your acceptance brings us one step closer."

He must be right because the beautiful crystal settles into my hand and my body glows with the same golden aura Jaxx and Kotah's did when they first held their soul shards.

Golden rays radiate from me like a pulsing wave of energy. My mates are ready for it and they grab hold of one another and then me. The connection of the five of us busts something open inside me. It's like a locked box of doubt and resistance inside me is obliterated and my lungs can expand to twice their volume. I can breathe again. Truly. Deeply. Breathe.

They are staring and I swipe at my eyes. "Sorry. I seem to have sprung a leak."

"Don't be sorry," Jaxx says, moving in for the group hug. "We've got you."

When his arms come around me and the others join in, my bond with the quint locks tighter into position. And I'm glowing like a pub sign. "Well, this is cool."

"You ain't seen nothin' yet," Jaxx says.

An hour later, with my stomach full, and the grand tour complete, we retire to the office to get everyone updated on where we are in our battles.

Jaxx and Calli start us off by telling us about Kotah's mentor visiting and bringing Raven into the spotlight. The cookies weren't drugged according to the lab tests, but Jaxx and Doc think there could still be reasons for a negative result. Or, maybe she was testing the waters and didn't want to tip her hand from the start.

The jury is still out on Raven.

I tell them what the Forest Lord said in my mind. "I wanted none of this Guardian. This is not my choice."

"You see," Hawk says, "this makes more sense to me. A creature as old and powerful as a Forest Lord has no reason to be involved in power struggles and plots for political gain. I believe someone is forcing his hand somehow."

Jaxx runs his fingers through his hair and the stuff falls perfectly back into place like it's been trained to do so. "How do we figure out who's doing it and how they've got him leashed?"

"I have a few ideas. Leave that with me."

I sigh, rubbing the top of Calli's thigh while she sits in my lap. No complaints here about there not being enough chairs in the office. "It would be great to not have to worry about him against us in the future."

"True story," Calli says. "He sounds terrifying."

"Brant," Hawk says. "You had a friend in billing at FCO that you trusted to look into me. Do you think she'd help us? After what happened to Jaxx's dad after he snooped into things, I hate to ask, but maybe she could come her and we could keep an eye on her."

"I can ask her. I'll call her tomorrow."

"Thanks. And Kotah, can we get access to Raven's incoming and outgoing calls? And maybe all calls related to the Bastion and the Fae Council? Oh, and did we ever find out when the plane was booked to come to Oregon and by who?"

"We can get anything you need, but that's going to be a lot of records to go through."

He nods. "Understood."

The ring of an incoming Zoom call has Jaxx leaning over to read the screen. "Hawk, it's Lukas."

He nods. "Brant, this one's for you, my man. Turn the monitor and open it up, Jaxx."

Jaxx opens the call and I've got three smiling faces staring at me. It's my kids… the three I made promises to before this all began. My heart expands and I have to take a few deep breaths or risk bawling like a baby again. "Hey, guys. It's good to see you safe."

*Calli*

I slide off Brant's lap and give him his moment. I could use one myself. These boys are my greatest strength and my greatest weakness all rolled up in one chaotic bundle. They trigger my emotions and if I succumb to the highs and lows, I'd be an emotional wreck most of the time.

Excusing myself, I step out onto the upstairs landing and head downstairs.

"You okay, kitten?" Jaxx says following me out.

"Mostly. I just need a minute. I'm going to go sit in the library and meditate for a bit."

"You want company?"

"I'm good, thanks. It's a lot sometimes, you know?"

Jaxx leans his elbows on the railing above and smiles. "I know. You do you, kitten. I love you."

"Love you too."

The library is a twenty-by-twenty-foot room with no windows, floor to ceiling bookshelves, and three rows of back to back bookshelves running down the center. In the corner farthest from the door, there's a leather chair and ottoman next to a reading lamp for those moments when one of us might want to escape.

Like now.

I leave the overhead light off and close the door, making my way to the reading nook. A month ago, I wouldn't have been able to maneuver the space without my hands out in front of my face.

Now, my phoenix senses get stronger by the day. My heightened vision, hearing, and sense of smell aren't as strong as the guys yet, but the sensory bombardment on top of the emotional turmoil is enough to shake my foundation some days. I find the chair, pull my knees up to my chest, and try to hold myself together.

Brant almost died last night. Hawk almost died last week. I was kidnapped the same night when Kotah was attacked by members of his own staff. And Jaxx, sweet Jaxx, almost died because of me. It's a lot.

*You can do this, girlfriend.*

I smile as Riley's pep talk comes right when I need it most. Figures. She always did know when I needed her. "I miss you, RiRi."

*I'm here for you.*

"Yeah, but you're not. I got Sonny for you. You didn't die for nothing."

*I didn't die, Cals. That was a body, a shell. We'll be together again soon.*

It's honestly too much to hope for. My mind's burping up what I need to hear when I need to hear it. "Why do I hear you so much clearer here?"

*I don't know where here is, but you're coming in loud and clear. I can't talk long though or they'll find me. Just know I'm fighting for you on this side.*

"What does that mean?"

*I've got your back. Always and forever. Heart you, huge.*

"Heart you more." As the presence in my mind drifts away, I close my eyes and sit in the silence that follows. Maybe Jaxx is right. If hearing pearls of encouragement from Riley makes things a little easier in the worst moments, what does it matter if it's real or not?

Riley is my anchor to the survivor I've always been.

I need to keep that part of me to become what the realms need in their phoenix. Some days it feels like too much and I want to curl up in a ball. Other days, when my mates are at my side and the universe seems to be rooting for us…

I think we just might get 'er done.

~ THE END ~

# AFTERWORD

I hope you loved Bear's Strength and getting to know Calli, Jaxx, Kotah, Brant, and Hawk better. If you want to help a girl out, leave a quick review or star rating on Amazon.

If you love these guys and want to make sure not to miss the fourth book, Hawk's Heart, you can find that on Amazon too.

# ABOUT THE AUTHOR

**Author Notes**
*Written on 07/25/2020*

Bear's Strength was a fun ride. I hope you loved Bear's Strength and getting to know Calli, Jaxx, Kotah, Brant, and Hawk better. If you'd like to leave a star rating or a couple sentences of a review on Amazon, I would love to read your thoughts.

Exciting news! Because so many fans have requested more, I've ordered a fifth cover and will write a fifth book in the series. Next up is Hawk's Heart, as planned. And following that will be… wait for it… Jaguar's Passion. I hope you love them all.

**Find Me**
My books - Amazon

Web page – www.jlmadore.com
Email – jlmadorewrites@gmail.com
Newsletter – JL Series Updates

# ALSO BY JL MADORE

Book 4 – Clash with the Magi Council

Book 5 – The Unstoppable Storme

## JL's More Traditional M/F, M/M, or Menage

### The Watchers of the Gray Series (Paranormal)
### Watchers of the Gray Boxset – Complete Series

Book 1 – Watcher Untethered – Zander

Book 2 – Watcher Redeemed – Kyrian

Book 3 – Watcher Reborn – Danel

Book 4 – Watcher Divided – Phoenix

Book 5 – Watcher United – Seth

Book 6 – Watcher Compelled – Bo

Book 7 – Watcher Unfeigned – Brennus

Book 8 – Watcher Exposed – Taharqa

### The Scourge Survivor Series (Fantasy)
### Scourge Survivor Series Boxset - Complete Series

Book 1 – Blaze Ignites

Book 2 – Ursa Unearthed

Book 3 – Torrent of Tears

Book 4 – Blind Spirit

Book 5 – Fate's Journey

Book 6 – Savage Love – epilogue novella

### Aliens of Atlantis Series (Sci-Fi)

Book 1 – Taryn's Tiderider

Book 2 – Kai's Captive

Book 3 – Alyandra's Shadow